DORA'S WORKHOUSE CHILD

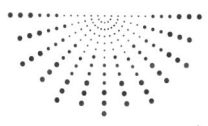

DOLLY PRICE

PUREREAD.COM

CONTENTS

Chapter 1	1
Chapter 2	5
Chapter 3	8
Chapter 4	10
Chapter 5	12
Chapter 6	17
Chapter 7	19
Chapter 8	22
Chapter 9	24
Chapter 10	27
Chapter 11	30
Chapter 12	34
Chapter 13	39
Chapter 14	41
Chapter 15	44
Chapter 16	50
Chapter 17	56
Chapter 18	60
Chapter 19	62
Chapter 20	65
Chapter 21	70
Chapter 22	72
Chapter 23	75
Chapter 24	78
Chapter 25	82
Chapter 26	86
Chapter 27	88
Chapter 28	92
Chapter 29	94
Chapter 30	96
Chapter 31	97
Chapter 32	100
Chapter 33	103
Chapter 34	105

Chapter 35	107
Chapter 36	112
Chapter 37	115
Chapter 38	117
Chapter 39	122
Chapter 40	125
Chapter 41	128
Chapter 42	130
Chapter 43	132
Chapter 44	134
Chapter 45	136
Chapter 46	138
Chapter 47	141
Chapter 48	145
Chapter 49	148
Chapter 50	152
Chapter 51	157
Chapter 52	159
Chapter 53	162
Chapter 54	164
Chapter 55	168
Chapter 56	173
Chapter 57	178
Chapter 58	180
Chapter 59	183
Chapter 60	185
Chapter 61	188
Chapter 62	192
Chapter 63	195
Chapter 64	198
Chapter 65	202
Chapter 66	204
Chapter 67	207
Chapter 68	210
Love Victorian Romance?	213
Our Gift To You	215

CHAPTER ONE

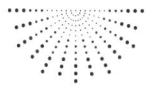

6th JUNE 1868

The porter threw the window open when he saw Dr. Pearse approach on his horse.

"You're too late, Doctor! A little girl, healthy, Mrs. Bateman says!"

Dr. Pearse felt that this June day might smile upon him after all. It was race-day, and he had money on *Double Trouble* in the three o'clock. He'd already had a drink or two for the journey when the messenger came saying that please, Doctor, Mrs. Marshall's time has come, and could he hurry. His assistant doctor was on leave. How had he let him go when Matron's baby was due? He concluded that age must be catching up with him.

"Excellent news, Wills!" said the doctor heartily. "I will go up and see her directly."

He tied up his horse at a post and ambled in, bag in hand, toward the main door of the Master's quarters, which was situated in a high octagonal structure at the center of six separate yards, like the cog on a wheel, with the walls between the yards like thick spokes. It was known as the Octagon, and on one of its floors, eight windows looked out on every part of the establishment, like a watchtower.

"Matron is sleeping," said Mrs. Bateman as she led him up three floors on the only good staircase in Blackbell Union Workhouse.

"I need not waken her, then," said the doctor, secretly delighted at his luck. "How is the baby?"

"She cried right off," was the reply. She led the way into the large bright area known as the Solarium. It was this space that had the eight windows, affording Master and Matron a view of all the workhouse buildings with their respective yards. Doctor took no notice today of the groups of people below, all in different yards separated by walls eight feet high and eighteen inches thick. It was after dinner in the workhouse; there was a brief period of recreation before work resumed. The men sat on steps or stood talking in groups; women, in striped blue uniforms, did the same; boys in their yard ran about throwing a ball blown up from a pig's bladder; girls in pinafores played tag and skipped with an old rope they'd found somewhere. A few more yards, attached to the Infirmaries and Nursery, were empty.

Down a hallway off the Solarium, Mrs. Bateman threw open the door to the Master's Apartments and led Dr. Pearse to the Master Bedchamber.

Doctor Pearse peered in the doorway at the sleeping mother and nodded.

"Better not wake her, if you're sure she's all right. Just bring the baby out to the parlor." he said, retreating, in case his very presence would ensure her awakening and therefore, at least a desultory examination.

Mrs. Bateman carried out the Moses basket, placed it on the table, and Doctor closed the door as quietly as ever he could.

"Oh, the pauper woman Davis was confined just after midnight." Mrs. Bateman said.

"Are mother and baby satisfactory?"

"Mother is fine. The baby took a few moments to breathe, was a bit blue, but at five minutes she was pink and bawling her head off."

Doctor's conscience stirred.

"Maybe I should have a look at her. But I'm in a bit of a hurry, Mrs. Bateman. If you could send over for her, it would be very convenient for me today rather than my walking over to the lying-in ward."

"Of course, Doctor. I'll run out and fetch her myself; that'd be quickest."

"I'll wait until you come back, to examine." Doctor said. He couldn't undo the ties at the backs of babies' gowns; that was a nurse's job. He sat down and lit his pipe.

"I won't be a moment then."

Mrs. Bateman went swiftly to the lying-in ward, where Dora Davis was cradling her baby girl. There was only one other patient there, an older mother, aged about thirty-eight, and three days delivered, whose baby had unfortunately died.

"Doctor is here and wants to examine her," Mrs. Bateman said, practically snatching the baby out of her arms and wrapping her up in an old grey blanket. "Oh! Matron had her baby, a girl it was, too!"

Dora watched her disappear with her infant. She lay back on the pillow. She felt exhausted. She would stay here for nine days; then she and the baby would go to the Nursery. The full weight of her situation began to weigh on her. How would she provide for her child? Would they remain in the workhouse, for the food and shelter it would afford, or would she leave the baby here and try to begin anew outside, unencumbered? Or would they both leave? Who would employ her? The father was gone, there would no help from anybody.

The baby was pretty with a little fair fuzz on her head. She'd named her Claretta.

CHAPTER TWO

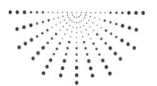

Mrs. Bateman was not at all surprised to see the doctor doing nothing except smoking his pipe. She laid the baby down in the basket.

"Now see here, Doctor, the pauper baby is on the left as you look into the cot. And the Marshall baby is on the right."

"Yes, yes, just strip them down to their clouts. No need for any more." Doctor Pearse did not want to risk a time-consuming nappy-change before the examination. He checked the watch hanging on his waistcoat. It was getting on for two o'clock. Mrs. Bateman's fingers deftly untied the back of Baby Marshall's gown.

"There, this one's ready." Mrs. Bateman picked up the Marshall baby and laid her on the table on a towel as Doctor Pearse laid his pipe aside.

The other infant began to wail as Mrs. Bateman gently undid her tiny gown and took her arms out of the sleeves.

"Pick her up, she'll wake Mrs. Marshall," said Doctor. Mrs. Bateman did as bidden, cuddling the newborn pauper in her arms, walking her about the parlour. As she did, she happened to glance out the window at the small private garden that was for the use of the Master's family.

"Well I never! There's young Lionel climbing the tree! Where's the servant got to? Get down, Lionel, get down at once!" she shouted out the window. "He doesn't hear me. I'll have to go down."

"Please do," said Doctor Pearse hastily, thinking that having to set a broken arm would put the kibosh on his afternoon completely. "I've finished this one, she's healthy." He laid her back in the basket and took the pauper's baby from Mrs. Bateman, before she rushed out.

He checked her well; listened to her heart and lungs, and her mouth and fingertips for any blueness, but was reassured as to her condition. He put her back into the cradle beside Baby Marshall, absently, to the right of her, and peered out the window to reassure himself that Lionel had four working extremities and an intact cranium and waited until Mrs. Bateman got back.

"The babies are in excellent condition," he said. "I have a pressing engagement, so if you don't mind, I will be upon my way." He stuffed the pipe back into his top pocket.

"Good luck," Mrs. Bateman said mischievously, as she began to dress one of the babies, the baby on the right into the soft flannel gown, wrapping her in the new white blanket, the baby on the left into the pauper's gown—greyed from many washings—wrapping her in the old blanket.

But he was already upon his way.

A few minutes later Dora sat up to receive her infant.

"Is she all right?" she asked anxiously, but in a low voice, conscious that the other woman had lost hers.

"She's healthy, nothing to worry about."

Dora put the baby to nurse, for she was awake and restless.

She was a little surprised that the baby had trouble suckling; this was her third feed and she'd had no trouble with the second. As she gazed down on the fuzzy head, it occurred to her that she seemed to have a little less hair than she'd thought.

CHAPTER THREE

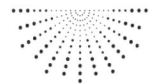

Mrs. Marshall stirred as the baby made a continuous wailing. "Mrs. Bateman?"

"I'm here, Matron. The doctor came, but you were sleeping, so he didn't want to wake you. He examined the baby; everything's normal."

"Thank God for that. Hand her to me, please, and pull back the curtains."

Mrs. Bateman picked up the bundle and placed her in Matron's arms. It was her first time holding her and getting a good look at her.

"She's a pretty one," said the mother. "Phoebe Jane."

"That's very nice, Matron."

A few moments later, the baby was feeding contentedly.

"Well, she knew what to do right away," said Matron, very pleased at the instant success. She felt very happy with herself.

"It's you, Matron. You have the right knack. And why not? Are you not a midwife too?"

CHAPTER FOUR

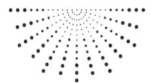

My baby had more hair, Dora said to herself. *The same shade as this, but a bit more of it*. She stared at the infant. She took the baby's hand in hers, the fingers were chubbier than she thought.

It was odd.

Dora remembered that on her baby's hip was a birthmark. She pulled down the top of her nappy to see. It was not there. As well as that, this child was quieter in her movements, her own baby had been more energetic, in spite of her slow start, she liked to kick and wave her arms about.

"They gave me the wrong baby back," she said, startled. "This is Matron's baby 'ere and she 'as mine!" Dora slipped out of bed and went to the door. An attendant came up the hall pushing a trolley of laundered bedlinen.

"Tell Nurse Bateman I want to see her." she said.

But it was ten o'clock that evening before Mrs. Bateman did her rounds.

"Nurse, this isn't my child." Dora said.

"Don't be ridiculous, of course it's your child! How could it not be your child?" Mrs. Bateman retorted.

"Easy, I got the wrong baby back. You mixed them up!"

Mrs. Bateman froze.

"That's not possible. The doctor and myself, we were very careful," she snapped. "Now I'm very busy." She walked away.

Dora found it hard to get to sleep, so anxious was she to right the error. As the ward became dark, her mind grew more active. She'd be able to tell them in the morning that her own baby had a birthmark, and there was no way she'd know that if it wasn't her own. The baby now with Matron would be checked for it and then she would have her own child back. First thing in the morning.

But as time wore on, other thoughts wandered into her mind. It occurred to her that if she left well enough alone, her child—her child born outside marriage, with no hope for her future beyond a scant education and an apprenticeship arranged by the Poor Law Guardians when she'd turn fourteen—could grow up in a family with all she needed and wanted, with a full stomach all her life, good clothes to wear instead of patched cast-offs, a father as well as a mother, toys and shoes, warm clothes in winter and above all, acceptance in society and respectability, and a good marriage too.

All it would need was for her to say nothing.

"You're Claretta now," she said, addressing the child with her. "You've drawn the short straw 'ere. You're going to be the pauper child. I'm sorry about it, but I'm not going to make a fuss. I'll look out for you as best I can while I'm in, but when I leave, you'll be 'ere alone. My own little girl is now Miss Marshall, and you're Claretta Davis, a workhouse child."

CHAPTER FIVE

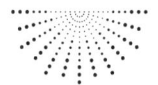

"Well done, my love," said the Master, Richard Marshall, planting a kiss on his wife's head. "I had no idea when I left this morning that I would return to our new addition."

Beryl gave him a cynical look.

"I told you I was getting pains."

"But of what use is a man at a time like that? Ah! I will surprise you. I won on a horse." He put his hand into his pocket and took out a bundle of notes.

"Five pounds!" she gasped.

"I think you will agree that Fortune smiled on us all today. I saw Dr. Pearse there. I pretended not to see him, and he pretended not to see me. I saw nobody from the Board. Though if I had happened to run into Braddish or Goulding, I would have been perfectly entitled to be there as much as they."

"Not when your wife was incapacitated. What if there'd been a crisis today? I could have hardly left my bed to go and see to it!"

"True, it was against the Rules. We were fortunate," said her husband. "And the Guardians never have to hear of it."

He glanced into the cradle at the sleeping infant.

"I declare she's the image of me. We will register her on Monday."

"And register the pauper's child. A girl too. Mrs. Bateman was here all day attending to me, and there was nobody in charge anywhere. I don't know if any rounds were done, or if prayers were said after supper."

"I'm sure Bateman stood in for us," said Richard. He was a rather rough, somewhat clumsy man. With his younger brother Daniel he had been a soldier in the Crimean War under Lord Raglan, and had risen to Sargeant. After the war he had tried many different occupations, not liking any until he'd been accepted as Master of this workhouse in a poor area near the London docklands.

The Crimea had changed Richard. He had returned unwounded in body but hardened in spirit; he became almost indifferent to suffering. The experience had the opposite effect on Daniel. He had lost a leg, and to his brother's amazement, his heart had become more tender, not angry. Daniel returned to live a simple, prayerful life and wanted little to do with material things, living in a cottage and earning his living by carpentry. The two brothers were still close, and though Richard thought that his brother was almost insane in his rejection of worldliness, he also acknowledged that he had a sort of uncommon insight, and he valued his opinion. Daniel was his conscience, when his conscience bothered him, which it did not do very often.

He excelled at organising, and managing the workhouse gave him satisfaction. He had to be very strict with the paupers. Though *The Duties of Master and Matron* had been well-read by him, he often said to himself that Poor Law Guardians lived in a world of their own making. They tended to regard most of the poor as deserving. If they saw what he had to put up with, they'd change their minds. Keep them always grateful, and a little hungry too, the adults, that was, for they were never supposed to be better off than the poorest working man outside.

"What was the name of the pauper who had the child?"

"Dora Davis."

"I predict that her child will be as hopeless as she."

"Oh, Richard. Where is your hope?"

"Hope is for dreamers, Beryl. She'll be just like her mother. Good night, sleep well." He stuffed the notes back into his pocket and left her.

Beryl lay down, and her heart filled with emotions she tried to keep herself from feeling. She wished she hadn't married such a man. By now, she knew his hardness of heart. But she had children, she reminded herself. Two beautiful children. Beryl always tried to look on the bright side of things.

She was a midwife, trained by a doctor, in her late thirties and lodging with an old couple nearby, the Talbots, while she responded to calls for her services in the area of the East End in which Blackbell was located. She'd lived with them for five years. She'd given up every hope of marriage and family. Richard was a friend of the Talbots and used to visit the house. He'd courted her. She'd felt flattered and grateful and more than ready to love him. She longed for a home of her own. Moving to the Blackbell Union Workhouse Master's Quarters was hardly her own establishment of course, but it was better than nothing, even if they did eat meals in the staff dining-room. But she insisted on a small range so that she could boil a kettle and cook simple dishes, at least, in the apartment. It was installed at their own expense.

Though she had had to go through an interview for the job as Matron, it had been just a formality, as the Guardians liked to have a married couple as Master and Matron, but not with young children, and they judged her childbearing years to be beyond her.

When Mr. Marshall had announced to them that he was about to become a father, the Board had been mildly displeased. But when he had informed them that another child was imminent, the Board had been annoyed. Though it was not forbidden to house a young family in the Master's Quarters, it was not encouraged, as the Matron in particular could neglect her duties to the Union Workhouse. She was responsible for the welfare of the females from seven to seventy or over, and of all boys and girls under seven; she supervised all the cutting-out and sewing of the inmates' rough uniforms, the kitchen and its cook and all matters dietary and domestic. She and Mrs. Bateman were the only midwives; but there were several trained nurses of which she had the charge. She was also supposed to deputise for the Master, if he was unavailable, and be able to manage the numerous account books and meticulous recording required by them. The Board of Guardians loved their account books and their clerk was required to pore over the entries of large and small expenses and report on them, so that they could see if they could pare them down anymore to spare the ratepayers, which included all of them of course.

Matron's servant, Annie, came in to see if she needed anything. Annie was not a pauper; they were not allowed to hire servants from the workhouse.

CHAPTER SIX

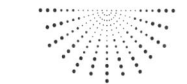

In a room several yards away, Mr. Bateman and his wife were settling down for the night.

"I've never had such a day as this," she said, taking the pins out of her hair. "I'm exhausted. At least tomorrow is Sunday. First the pauper goes into labour, and I was up all night with her, and then Mrs. Marshall after that. On top of that, I had all the cares that Matron attends to. Are you listening to me, Wills Bateman?"

"Yes, dear."

"You haven't heard a word I said, as usual," she nudged him. "Did you see Doctor Pearse on his way back from the races?"

"Yes, dear."

"And did his horse come in?"

"No. He was the worse for wear. Very drunk. I hope nobody needs him here during the night."

Beryl settled into bed.

"He was tipsy when he was here, examining the babies."

Her husband had already fallen asleep. It annoyed her that this man, who did hardly anything all day except to let people in and out the workhouse gate, could fall asleep so easily, while her mind always jumped around with the activities of the day. As she finally closed her eyes, her mind drifted to something that was said to her by the pauper mother.

"Oh no," she groaned. "It can't be. I'll have to find that out first thing in the morning."

Not a mile away, Doctor Pearse was climbing into his bed in his rooms. He'd lost ten shillings on *Double Trouble.* He'd never again listen to a tip from Phipps, his barber. Or, rather, he'd never eavesdrop when Phipps was giving tips to his other clients. He hadn't asked him directly because he didn't want anybody to know he liked a flutter.

He took a powder for his aching head. At least he had not been needed for the deliveries at the Union Workhouse, and no emergency had called him there. Apart from losing, he'd enjoyed the day.

As he closed his eyes, a memory from the day drifted into his head, he saw himself place the second baby, the pauper's baby, in the cot to the right of the Master's baby. That was correct, wasn't it? That was what Mrs. Bateman had said . . . was it? Never mind. No need to worry. If it was incorrect, she would have known right away, and reversed his error. No need to worry . . . he pulled his nightcap down over his eyes and drifted off to sleep.

CHAPTER SEVEN

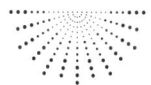

The following morning Nurse Bateman marched straight to the lying-in ward after coming on duty. She dreaded the interview. There could be hell to pay. But she, at least, was completely innocent. She'd had to go and get Lionel out of the tree, and Dr. Pearse should have paid more attention. She had explicitly told him. But he'd had drink on his breath. She'd be prepared to state that too.

"You told me something last evening that worried me," she said to Dora Davis, who was sitting up in bed holding the baby.

"Oh, never mind what I said, Nurse." Dora replied. "I was tired."

"Are you sure then?" Mrs. Bateman felt relieved, and not at all inclined to pursue the matter further.

"I'm sure. Never mind." Dora looked down and stroked Claretta's head.

"Well, then. As if I hadn't enough on my mind yesterday, I had to bear the worry of *that*."

"I'm sorry," Dora said.

"That's all right then. I'll send Polly in with your medicine. How are you today, Martha?" she asked the other patient.

"Apart from not 'aving my child alive? I suppose I'm all right."

"I only asked, Martha." Mrs. Bateman glowered. She still felt very fatigued. She was going to have to do double-duty until Matron was back. She left the room.

"You are a clever one," Martha said to Dora, smiling quietly.

"Clever, what do you mean?"

"I know. I know what you did."

"I did nothing at all. They did it."

"I 'eard you, last night, talking about drawin' the short straw. If I was you, I might have said noffink either, maybe. Are you going to be good to that one?" She nodded toward the infant.

"Of course!" Dora was indignant.

"If you gets tired of 'er, I'll be 'er second mother." She looked longingly at the infant.

"I'm sorry yours didn't live," Dora said. "It must be hard for you to have to share the room with me. Were you in love with the father?"

"I was married to 'im, love, if that means I was in love with him. He died three months ago."

"Oh, I'm sorry to hear that. Was 'e sick long?"

"He got stomick fever in Newgate, cholera I say. What about you?"

20

"I was in love with 'im. Still am. But he was from Prussia and he don't know nothin' about the baby. My father threw me out. Said he'd lose customers."

"Russia, did you say?"

"No, Prussia, a different place! It's near Austria-'Ungary! That's 'ow he explained it to me. He's half-'Ungarian."

"What's your father's trade?"

"Fishmonger. He has a stall in Blackbell Market. Soon as I began to show, I was gone. Kept myself for a while on a few shillings 'e gave me, and then I came in 'ere."

"And what was the baby's father's trade? Was 'e a sailor? What if he comes back and wants to marry you? You've given away his child now."

"Shhh! Never say that!" She instinctively covered Claretta's head again. "I might never see 'im again. He was with a circus —an acrobat. I did very well by our girl, if I might say so. Our daughter will grow up with all she needs. You not goin' to tell nobody about 'er, are you?"

"Naw. Why would I?"

"My only worry is, that Nurse Bateman will remember seein' the birthmark when my baby was born, if she did see it, I know she's forgot it now. What if she saw it, and remembers?"

"I think she'll say noffink. The longer it goes on, the more trouble it would make, if she was to say anyfink."

"It was only a light mark, 'ardly noticeable really."

"Well there you are then, she probably din't see it at all, so don't worry."

CHAPTER EIGHT

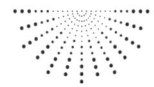

On Monday, Dr. Pearse called to see Mrs. Marshall and was satisfied that she was recovering well. He told her that he found no abnormality with her baby, the infant was fine in every respect.

"You saw the birthmark, Dr. Pearse?"

"Oh, yes, yes."

"What did you think of it?"

"Let me have another look," he said skillfully. "Ah! A little *'café au lait.'* There's nothing to worry about. Should fade with time. Lucky it's not on her face, eh?"

After he left the apartment, he began to walk toward the Male Infirmary.

He had not seen the birthmark before, but then he had not fully examined the children. Again, he hoped that the infants were returned to the right mothers. The pauper mother would surely know if there had been an error, for her child had been with her all day and she'd have gotten a good look at her and noticed a birthmark if it had been there.

That settled that, then. His mind was eased before he went to see his patients in the dim, poorly ventilated Infirmary.

A few days later, Martha prepared to leave the lying-in ward to return to the Women's Wing.

"I'll miss you," said Dora. They had become good friends. She felt sorry for Martha. She'd had eight children, and none had survived except a boy who had gone to sea.

"And I'll miss you, and that little one," Martha said. "You don't tek her up enough when she cries. Do a little better with her if you want to pass yourself off as her rightful Ma."

Dora and the baby would soon join the other mothers and infants in the Nursery.

"Why don't you ask to work there?" Dora said. "Then you could tek her up as much as you please, while I'm working. But if I was you, I'd leave here if I 'ad a chance."

"Anytime I left before, I was sorry," said Martha. "So here I'll stay. I prefer it to not knowing where the next meal is comin' from, or from sleepin' on wet grass. I'll ask Matron when she comes back, if I can work in the Nursery. You know you'll be put to pickin' oakum?"

"What? They do tha' here? I thought that was for criminals."

"Your crime is you 'ave a child and you not married."

"What is it exactly, oakum?"

"It's old rope, 'orrible, you have to pick it all apart to a single thread. They never run out of it neither."

CHAPTER NINE

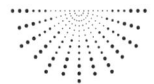

"Will you be fit to return to work tomorrow, Beryl?" asked her husband after fourteen days had gone since little Phoebe had arrived. "You are greatly missed."

Matron dreaded going back to work. But duty called. There would be a backlog of work to be done. Annie would look after the children, bringing the baby over to her office when it was time for her feed.

She was curious to see the child who had been born the same day as her little Phoebe, so she went to the Nursery first.

Dora had been expecting this moment, the morning when Matron would come in to see her and the infant that she did not know was her own.

After greeting her, Matron looked directly into the cot and took the baby up, holding her in front of her in the light. Dora's heart was in her mouth, but Matron was simply examining the child with a professional eye.

"She looks healthy enough," was her verdict, before placing the infant down again and wrapping her with speed and efficiency.

"Is your own baby well?" asked Dora, hoping her voice betrayed nothing of what she was feeling, beyond a polite concern.

"Very well! She's a busy little baby, always waving arms or legs, as if she can't bear to be still. Is this little one quiet?"

"Very placid."

"Mine keeps me awake all night. Well I must get on." Matron turned to go. "We have a woman in labour in the Receiving Ward. Never a dull moment."

"I was going ter ask you, Matron, a favour, if you don't mind."

"What is it? Quickly. I'm very busy."

"Could Martha Ballard, whose child died, come and work in the Nursery?"

"Well I don't know about that. Why?"

"I feel sorry for 'er and she loves children. Eight died."

Matron made no reply, but Dora saw her eyes soften.

"What did you name your child, by the way?"

"Claretta."

Matron thought it too fancy a name for a girl who would be apprenticed out; mistresses liked servants to have plain names. It would be better if she were Annie, or Elizabeth shortened to Betty, but she couldn't think of a short name for Claretta except Clara which was just as uppity.

"How did you think of that name? It's quite unusual," she said, while Dora smiled to herself.

"I read it in a romantic story." Dora said, thinking of her Prussian acrobat, whose sister's name was Claretta. Dora had thought it the prettiest name she had ever heard. She had never read a story, and she could only write her name.

Matron sighed and turned to go. Foolish girls! But then, she too had been taken in by foolishness. How had she, in her wildest dreams, thought Richard Marshall a Prince Charming?

CHAPTER TEN

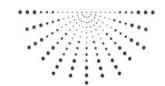

TWO YEARS LATER

This is the last day I shall pick this oakum, thought Dora with delight, regarding her hardened fingertips. She was in the Nursery workroom.

"Where are you going, when you go out?" asked a woman named Wilma.

"I 'ave to go back to my father's. He's talkin' to me again. He has nobody to 'elp him."

"Why don't you take her with you?"

"No, I can't. We'd be back here in no time, the two of us."

"Not if you live wiv your father, you won't."

"While he accepts me, I don't think he'll accept 'er."

"You don't have to worry about her 'ere, Martha loves 'er as much as you do, don't she?"

"She's like her second mother," said Dora.

She threw the unfinished oakum back into a barrel. She looked forward to being out again, meeting people, going where she pleased, earning money, buying ribbons to make her old clothes look new and pretty, and getting out of this ugly shapeless uniform. She had no worries about Claretta, who at two years, was weaned. She'd have gone long ago only for Martha, who lectured her that the baby would die if she was weaned early and kept her to it. Claretta would be in the Nursery until she was three, and then move to the Children's Wing.

She'd miss her a little, she admitted. But she'd miss even more glancing furtively up to the Solarium to see if Annie was at a window, with Phoebe in her arms, looking out to show her the people below, as an amusement. She was sometimes lucky. She saw a fair-haired child, squirming, reaching out of the confines of whoever's arms were holding her. She seemed very keen to join what was an active world below her. Once, she seemed to reach out her arms to Dora, or maybe that was her fancy.

If only you knew, little Phoebe!

She returned to the main room. Martha was bathing Claretta in a basin set on the table. The little girl's hair had turned darkish, she now looked very different to Phoebe. She was small but sturdy, had a plump face, big blue eyes and a sweet smile with dimples.

What was done was done. And for the best, thought Dora, as she bid her goodbye the following day, knowing that Martha supplied all the love that her child needed.

"Mamma will be back soon," she lied in the universal way that mothers do when bidding their children goodbye for any length of time, not to mind forever.

Claretta waved *bye-bye*, with a dimpled smile.

Dora walked out the workhouse gates in her own clothes and resolved she would never come back. She gave one last, lingering glance at the Octagon where her own child lived. There was nobody at the windows today. She bid her child a silent *Goodbye and God bless,* blinked back a tear, and hastened on.

CHAPTER ELEVEN

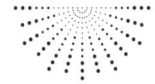

Matron sank down on the sofa and took the child on her lap. Phoebe immediately began to scramble her way down again.

"Miss Phoebe never stops." remarked Annie. She was going to add: *I don't know where you got her,* in the casual way that people do, but remembered the rumours just in time.

"I wish she'd sleep at night." Beryl said. "She never needs more than four hours at a time. I've often been tempted to send her over to the Nursery so that I could get a full night, but Mr. Marshall would never allow it, and rightly so. Do you know what she did last night? She climbed over the top of her cot. Her toddler cot! I awoke and caught her just in time. I don't know what we will do. You may go, Annie, and have a good day off tomorrow."

"I hope you have a nice time with Miss Eldred, Matron."

The following day Beryl welcomed her sister Jane Eldred from the train. She was going to stay three weeks. She had never seen Phoebe before and was looking forward to the meeting immensely. They all returned to the apartments, where Beryl made a cup of tea and warmed up currant scones in the range oven.

"So, who do you think she's like?" she asked, as Phoebe, sitting on her lap, played with a cup and spoon.

"I can't tell. She's reddish-fair; no Eldred has hair that colour. Maybe in Richard's family?"

"They're all dark, like us."

"She has a little elfin face, hasn't she? And dancing eyes! So dark and soft, they put me in mind of black velvet."

"Yes. I think she'll be very pretty. She hasn't my square face! She'll have more admirers than I! Oh, all right, Phoebe, you can go then." She set the child on the floor.

"She can't rest for a moment. No wonder she's thin! Lionel, as you see, is quite chubby." The little boy looked up from his toy soldiers and smiled happily.

Phoebe toddled over to him and felled his row of soldiers, which he only laughed at, then she stood and pulled herself up on a chair, sitting there chuckling, before she got to her feet and attempted to climb the high chairback. The chair began to keel over. Beryl was on her feet with haste. Phoebe was lifted to safety.

"She has no fear!"

"Get a baby cage, Beryl."

"We have one. She can reach the top bars and pull herself up, and I'm afraid she'll topple out."

The following day, Jane accompanied Beryl on her rounds at eleven o'clock. The workhouse interior had a dismal look, with small windows set high in the walls. She saw the day rooms where the elderly sat, and the dormitories with their rows of plain (ugly, she thought) beds. She marvelled at the mountains of laundry in the Wash-house and silently deplored that boys of ten or so were operating the mangler; it was hard, dangerous work. The kitchens were very large, much of the produce came from the kitchen-gardens. The Infirmaries were crowded, busy and odiferous. Then Beryl took her to see the Nursery.

The first person she saw was a child who, in the way she turned her head and smiled with dimples each side of her mouth, reminded her instantly not only of her own sister, but of their mother. Beryl was telling her about the various children in sight, and finally came to the dark-haired child.

"Claretta was born the same day as Phoebe," she said, lifting the child from the floor into her arms. Jane was dumbfounded. Seeing their faces together, she saw a strong resemblance. It made her feel uncomfortable as a dreadful suspicion entered her mind. *Did nobody else see this?*

"Her mother left some time ago. Left her in our care. The Ratepayers are her parents now. She and all the girls here will go into service. The boys will have apprenticeships." She put the child down again.

An inmate moved and swept Claretta up in her arms, and saying something about her needing her nose wiped, bore her away.

Martha wiped Claretta's nose even though it was clean. She'd seen the dumbfounded look on Matron's sister's face. Claretta was hers. She was Martha's child now, and her worst nightmare would be if she were taken away! They must never find out.

Jane left without saying anything about her suspicions. But it troubled her. She'd seen Claretta again, on purpose, gone over to the Nursery a few times. One of the women there was very fond of the child and seemed to spirit her out of her sight whenever she appeared, which raised her suspicions even more.

As the train pulled out of Victoria Station, Jane pondered all. But she could not bring herself to mention anything to her sister. She could hardly mention it to herself! It was too, too awful if true!

CHAPTER TWELVE

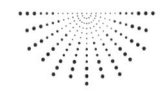

"Don't want to go to Chillen's Wing!" pouted Claretta.

"I'll come an' see you, luv! There now, don't fret." Martha wiped the tears from the little girl's eyes. In truth she felt close to tears herself but blinked them back.

Claretta would soon be too old for the Nursery. She was to join the boys and girls in the Under-7 Wing. Martha hoped she would get permission to visit her, but nothing was sure. She was not the child's mother. But Matron, a mother herself, might understand. Martha was always a little afraid to bring Claretta to Matron's attention. She'd never told a soul what she knew.

There had been no communication from Dora Davis.

Occasionally she saw Dora's child, who, now being a little girl, was taken for walks outside the workhouse. Martha occasionally went outside on a Sunday. When Claretta would begin school, the schoolmistress would take her out for walks too. It would be her very first time outside the walls. For now, her outside world was the tall brick wall enclosing the Nursery yard. There were dandelions and daisies pushing themselves up through the cracks in the ground, and she delighted in them. An occasional butterfly filled with bright colour made its way into the yard and enchanted her and the other little ones.

Whenever Martha went outside, she brought back bunches of wild flowers to the Nursery. Apart from a few old toys lying about, the toddlers had little to amuse them. They played with gnawed wooden bricks and big buttons. They were well-fed—Matron made sure of that, but except at Christmas, treats were almost unheard of. Matron's requests for more toys and picture-books for the Nursery were nearly always turned down by the Board of Guardians.

On Claretta's third birthday, Matron arranged for her to come up to the Octagon for a piece of Phoebe's birthday cake. Her servant Annie was sent to bring her there, and Claretta did not want to go, for Annie was a stranger. She cried and kicked as she was carried off.

Annie knew the child was frightened. She tried to reassure her, but her screams did not cease. Annie was not fond of pauper children and was relieved to hand her to Matron.

Matron thought it was a shame she could not have asked Martha Ballard to bring her over, but it was a strict rule that inmates did not enter the Octagon. She felt the failure of the scheme before it even began.

Phoebe came running over.

"Have cake!" Claretta said.

"Stop crying!" said Phoebe then, a little imperiously.

"Phoebe, be kind," said her mother, Claretta in her arms. Matron, with the skill of her years of nursing, was able to soothe the child, and soon she was sitting at the table, her tears dried on her cheeks, which were instead smeared with crumbs as she ate. Lionel was beside her and he kindly encouraged her to eat it all up.

The door opened and Mr. Marshall walked in.

"Papa!" cried Phoebe, running to him. He swept her up in his arms.

"How is my little tumbler today?"

"Papa! Papa! I want to jump! Will you catch me?"

"You know I don't like this, Richard."

"There's no danger." Mr. Marshall set his daughter on top of a cupboard which was the height of his shoulder. She stood up, her face lit with anticipation as he took several steps backward.

"You're too far away," warned Matron.

"Nonsense!"

"Now, Papa!" With a joyful cry, Phoebe launched herself through the air to be caught by him.

Claretta laughed. She thought Phoebe was a funny little girl.

"Again, Papa!" she held up her arms to him to be lifted up again.

"No, no, Phoebe, Papa wants cake!" He laughed heartily.

Matron wished her husband would not encourage Phoebe in these wild capers. Someday she would have a serious accident. And Lionel was left in the shade, though he loved and admired his little sister. Phoebe had her father and Lionel wrapped around her little finger. But Mr. Marshall gave more attention to his daughter than to his son, and Matron was concerned about it, for Lionel's sake.

Then Mr. Marshall's eye caught the pauper child, in her drab little frock, sitting at his table.

"What is this, Mother?" he asked sternly.

"This is the girl who was born the same day as our Phoebe. I brought her up for cake. I told you, Richard."

"You told me that she was going to have cake, but not that she was to be brought up here for it. You know what this does, Mother. The inmates see our rooms, modest as they are, and it makes them discontented and ungrateful."

"But she's a baby yet! How could she have cake in the Nursery, with all the other children looking on, with no cake for them? I thought you understood she would be coming over here, Richard."

"A pauper child. Not only a pauper, but illegitimate. I could use a worse word, but don't want our children to learn it."

"Pauper, illegitmit!" echoed Phoebe.

Claretta began to feel fearful again. She did not know the Master of the Workhouse, and he seemed big and frightening.

"You had better take her back, Annie," said Matron quietly. "To the Nursery, for another few days."

"If she is three today, she goes to the Children's Wing today." Her husband laid down the law. "That is the Rule. I'm surprised at you, Mother." He sat down and motioned to her to cut him a piece of cake. "Why haven't you fostered her out?"

"Because her own mother was with her for two years. And then, it would be cruel to send her away, when she was used to the Nursery maids. You should leave these matters to my judgement, Richard."

"Life is hard for paupers, Beryl. They should learn from the first, that life is harsh. You should not spoil a pauper child."

Beryl swallowed her rising anger. Was she always to live under his domination, his cold heart? As Annie took Claretta's hand and led her away, Beryl gave her a look of pity. Claretta was looking back at her. In that glance, they communicated a mutual feeling of helplessness, a kind of common feeling, she thought.

CHAPTER THIRTEEN

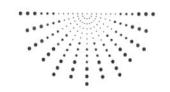

Planted suddenly into a place where she was a stranger and everybody a stranger to her, Claretta was very unhappy. She sat on a bench at suppertime and left her bread soaked in milk untouched. She wanted Auntie Martha.

"What's your name?" asked a bigger boy sitting next to her.

"Claretta."

"Her name is Claretta," he said to a girl beside him.

"Are you new?" he asked then, while the girl beside him leaned forward to get a better look at her around him. She was smiling at her.

"I want Auntie Marfa."

"Who's Auntie Marfa?" asked the girl. She had nice long, fair hair and smiling eyes.

"Come on now, eat yer supper," said an old woman who was suddenly beside her. She put a spoon to her mouth. Claretta took it with reluctance, looking about her fearfully, at the long tables and the children seated there, at the women going about, one of them angry with a crying child who wouldn't eat. She opened her mouth obediently to receive the spoon offered to her by the old woman. The boy and girl played with her after supper. Later, she went to sleep in a big room with many beds and fell asleep.

Claretta was cheered the following morning by the appearance of the Matron, for every day of her life, she saw her as she did her rounds. She was not new, like everybody and everything else today. Matron spoke kindly to her and patted her head.

The boy and girl who had spoken to her yesterday played with her again. They were nice. He said he was Thomas, and his sister's name was Alice. In the middle of the morning, their mamma came in and took them away, but they came back. Alice was crying and Thomas was trying to comfort her.

CHAPTER FOURTEEN

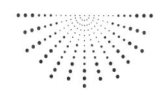

Phoebe broke her collarbone when she was six years old after falling out of a tree. But while Phoebe was disconsolate for a while, after she healed, she simply took up where she had left off, and her mother was the disconsolate one, fearing daily that she would hurt herself, while Annie was convinced that one day she'd injure herself and be a cripple.

Lionel had gone away to school, and the plan was that Phoebe should be enrolled also, in a school for girls, preferably a country school where she could be outside a great deal. Perhaps the discipline of a school would tame her. She could not sit still.

Matron thought about the other girl born on Phoebe's birthday. Claretta Davis would move from the Children's Wing to the Girls' Wing on her seventh birthday, which was coming up soon. She had not had any birthday cake since that unlucky visit several years ago. Martha, from the Nursery, had the same permission as any parent to visit her, once weekly. Mr. Marshall did not know that. He was a stickler for the rules and would put a stop to it without delay.

Thankfully he did not care to walk about in her jurisdiction very often.

He came in just as she was sewing one of his buttons back on a shirt. He had attended a Board of Guardians Meeting, and she expected to be briefed upon his return from the Boardroom on the second storey.

"Well, Mother," he said in his usual greeting. "I will have a Birthday Surprise for our little girl."

"What is that?" she bit off the thread.

"Have you ever heard of Victor Ahlers? No? As I had not either, before today. Goulding and Braddish were talking of him. He has a famous Touring Circus, which will be coming to Town next month! He's renowned for his tightrope walkers and trapeze artists. They are said to be fearless and daring. Especially an artiste named the *Amazing Aleksander*."

"A circus! Phoebe will like it, and Lionel will be at home by then."

"Precisely my thought! We'll take the evening off, both of us —the Batemans will cover the rounds—and we'll hire a cab and all of us go. It will be quite an excursion."

"Oh Richard, I will look forward to that greatly!" her eyes shone. "I only hope that Phoebe won't want to emulate them, after we get home! She quite frightens me, as you know."

"The collarbone gave me a start also, but I love her fearless quality, Mother."

"Richard, could you not call me *Mother* when the children are not here? I don't mind when they are. But why call me *Mother* when we're alone?"

"I suppose it's just habit," he said. "Very well then, Beryl. I shall try to remember. By the way, you do look very nice tonight. That shade of blue suits you."

"Why, thank you, Richard." She felt pleased at the thought of their having an outing. They could not take their holidays together, which was a great annoyance. And often she wished she didn't work with her husband. If she was angry with a decision he made about the workhouse, she carried her anger home.

She attended the Guardians Meetings, but not every week. It took too much time out of her day, and some of the meeting was devoted to discussing horses, guns, and coming entertainments. For once, she was happy that he had news of a kind to benefit her and the family.

CHAPTER FIFTEEN

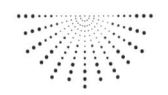

Claretta walked to the Girls' Wing clutching her one possession, her doll. She was feeling quite grown up. She saw her friend Alice almost immediately. A year older, Alice had moved last year. Her brother Thomas had lived in the Boys' Wing for two years.

She'd seen Martha yesterday. Martha had combed her hair and plaited it for her. She hoped the women in this House she was going to would not cut it off. She'd seen children with all the hair cut off, and they looked dreadful. Martha had given her a birthday present, a doll made of straw, clothed in a spotted pinafore, with blue buttons for eyes and a curved line of stitches for her smiling mouth. It was the first doll she had ever owned, and she loved her. She'd named her Ruth after the girl in the Bible. She liked Bible stories.

The yard was full of girls older than she. How funny it was to be the oldest child yesterday in the Childrens' Wing, and the youngest today in this one! She knew some of them, but Alice was the one she knew best.

"Claretta!" Alice ran to her. "Come on, I'll show you everything! I hope we can sit together at supper. What a lovely doll! I had a doll—a long time ago. Her name was Belinda."

"Did you lose her?" asked Claretta.

"She went up in the fire along with everything," said Alice.

"Oh, I'm sorry." She knew that there had been a dreadful fire in Alice's house when she was a little girl, and her father had died in it. Then her family had to come into the workhouse. She wondered what it was like not to live in a workhouse. She knew nothing of the outside. Thomas and Alice had told her about a lot of very astonishing things, like shops. If you had money, you could buy anything at a shop. Anything you wanted. You could buy ten dolls at a shop if you had the money, but you had to have the money. She'd seen money—pennies, farthings, even sixpences, which was a lot of money. Martha had shown them to her. Outside, she was sure, was a very strange place and she was curious. Martha had told her of a place she had gone to where there was grass all around, and many, many flowers. A park. People were sitting on the grass, eating their dinner. It was another world, like Heaven, maybe. There were little tufts of grass here and there in the yards, but nobody sat on it, and as for eating—you could only eat at a table with a lot of other people, not outside. She tried to imagine the yard covered in green grass and bright, colourful flowers and could not.

She knew birds. They flew into the yards. She loved them. She knew their names. The robin was her favourite. She had made a friend of a robin, once. She'd kept crumbs for him in her pinny pocket. He'd hopped very near to her to get the crumbs. He'd come back every day that summer, and the next one too. After eating the crumbs, he had flown away, to the outside, where he could see a lot of different things. She wished a robin could talk so he could tell her all about outside.

She knew people outside dressed differently too, because sometimes visitors came in and she had seen them—ladies in dresses of all colours and big hats with ribbons and feathers on them.

Claretta knew that her home was a Union Workhouse, but up to recently she had never fully understood that not everybody lived in workhouses. When Alice and Thomas had told her that their house had burned down, she thought it was a workhouse, a great, big place like this. But Martha one day had explained to her that no, the Winters had lived in a *house*. One day, Martha had taken her to the top floor of their wing, stood up on a stool and lifted her up to the high window so that she could see houses. They were small; she didn't know how very many people could fit in them. Martha told her that every house had a man, a woman, and a few, maybe two or five perhaps, children living there. It was called a family. They all lived and ate together, with no walls separating them, but a wall separated them from the next family in the next house. That's if they were rich. Poor families lived in a room, with another family in the next room, and maybe six families to a house.

Claretta took in the information with great interest. How strange it was! Martha went on to tell her that some houses had grass and flowers outside instead of yards. Grass and flowers. A house with little parks! Claretta thought of them with a certain longing. *Shops and parks!*

"Will I ever see 'em?" she'd asked Martha, excitedly.

"I'm sure you will. When you begin school, the schoolmistress will tek you for walks now and then. Then you'll see many houses an' all sorts."

Claretta pondered this. She was looking forward to going to school, though she was sure she'd be frightened of the schoolmistress, Miss Penworth, and the other teacher who would teach them how to work, Mrs. Tate.

Now, in the Girls' Wing, she looked around the yard.

"What are they doing?" she asked Alice, pointing to a group of girls.

"Skipping! When they've finished with the rope, it'll be our turn! I'll teach you!"

School began for Claretta the very next day. She entered the classroom fearfully, and saw Miss Penworth, a tall woman who asked her name, wrote it in a very big book, and directed her to sit at a table at the front, with several other children. Claretta obeyed. Soon, she learned to chant some letters. Everybody else chanted them very well, but she did learn A, B, C, D, E and after that she was lost and could not do the remainder, but Miss Penworth didn't seem to mind when she fell silent.

The girl beside her was named Julia, and she showed her how to do things. She also began to learn numbers. She could count to ten, from listening to others. Her first day of education went very well and she was pleased with herself, and Miss Penworth, she discovered, was kind. Some of the bigger children—very big at twelve and thirteen—were writing their names on the blackboard and doing sums, and she wondered if she would ever be able to do them too.

The classroom had big windows and plenty of light. After school, Mrs. Tate put a duster in Claretta's hands and told her to dust the window sills. She did her best, but not fast enough, and left a cobweb in a corner—and Mrs. Tate was angry, and told her she would have to learn how to do it fast, and properly.

"You're to be 'prenticed out, you'll have to know how to work," she said with severity, taking the duster from her and showing her how to sweep broad strokes across the sill, catching up cobweb and spider. She flung the duster back at her.

Prenticed out? What did she mean? Claretta felt apprehensive as she tried to copy the long broad strokes she had seen Mrs. Tate do. But her arms were too short to do the same. Still, Miss Tate was gone now and Claretta could hear her angry voice address someone else.

Was she to leave the workhouse then, for it seemed like it, and she had to know how to dust a windowsill before she left. But what about school? She liked school. She was reassured by Abbie Graves, a bigger girl, that she would not leave until she was fourteen years old. That was a long, long way off.

School was to close for the summer in a few days, but before that, there was to be a great treat. Miss Penworth was going to take them outside for a walk! Claretta was so excited she could hardly wait. They walked out of the classroom straight onto a gravel path, with trees on either side, and came to the big gate, which Mr. Bateman opened for them. And then, they were outside! Marching along the path, Claretta became aware of people stopping to look at them. She did not know why that was.

"Workhouse children." she heard somebody say.

"Paupers, go back inside!" hooted a rude boy, to the laughter of his friends.

Perhaps outside was not so nice after all. But they came to a corner, and when they went 'round it, Claretta saw a row of neat houses, inside iron gates. She stopped to peer inside the gate of one of them.

"Claretta Davis, what are you doing?" asked Miss Penrose. "It's very rude to look in somebody's gate!"

Claretta coloured. "I only wanted to see the little park with the flowers," she said lamely.

There was a titter from the older girls.

"It's called a *garden*," said one of them. They walked on.

"That's where Doctor Pearse lives," said Annie, nudging her to look at a house covered in ivy.

"Does his family live there too?"

"No, he's not married. Now, look we're coming to Mr. Braddish's house. Miss Penworth will stop us all, and she will tell us about it."

Sure enough, Miss Penworth made them stop walking, and she waved to a large gate, inside of which they could easily see a large garden and an elegant house with high chimneys.

"Mr. Braddish is a member of the Board of Guardians. Julia Grey, what is the Board of Guardians?"

"It's the group of kindly gentlemen who pay for us to live in the workhouse, with food and board and education." said Julia.

"Yes. And you should all be very grateful to be so well cared for by the Board of Guardians, girls. Let us go on."

She saw many other new things that day. But they had not passed a *shop!* How she longed to see a shop!

CHAPTER SIXTEEN

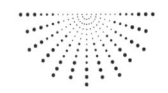

"**D**ora Davis!"

Dora spun around to see her friend Nancy behind her as she neared the box office.

"You look so elegant tonight, Dora, so sporty with that feather in your 'at! I thought you'd come 'ere! Still got a spark left for the *Amazing Aleksander*?"

"Nance, you silly old wagon, where've you been?"

"I been down on my luck. That's where I've been!"

"I'll treat you. Two sixpenny seats, please."

"*The Amazing Aleksander*." Nancy said. "Is back in town, and I heard his sister is tourin' as well."

"Claretta?" Dora had not uttered the name in years. It felt strange on her tongue.

"You and he 'ad a little fling, din't you?"

"Yes, you know we did."

"An' you disappeared for a while, din't you."

"I disappeared for a long while," Dora said. "It seems like a long time ago, now—I—"

She stopped suddenly, dropped her head and led Nancy away quickly.

"What is it? What's the matter, Dora? You look ill."

"I'm no' ill," Dora recovered herself and peeped around Nancy's shoulder. "Just some people I din't expect to see 'ere, that's all. I don't think they'd know me, but just in case . . ."

Nancy looked around and followed her gaze. She saw a family, a father, mother, and their two children, a boy about ten years old and a red-blonde girl about six or seven on their way in. The girl was restless and looking about her with wide, fascinated eyes.

Dora was staring at the girl.

"That's why I went away, over there, see, the little girl. She's my daughter, and Aleksander's. She's going in there to see 'im and she won't have any knowledge that the acrobat she's watchin' is her own father! Fancy!"

Phoebe was so excited in the Big Top she could not stop prattling. Though the band played lively music, she chattered above it to her father who was beside her, until he asked her to please, please desist if she had any regard for his ears. She sat on the bench, staring up at the ropes, ladders, poles, and other paraphernalia. Then the lights were put out, and with a puff of smoke that seemed to come from nowhere, causing exclamations of surprise, the Show began. There was a loud bang and flashing lights, and the ring was lit up. The Ringmaster appeared amid a circle of white horses with a young woman standing upon the back of each. Each girl wore a shining, short costume. Phoebe had never seen anything like it, but to her astonishment, that was only the beginning of her surprise. One by one, the girls began to dance and pirouette on the horses' backs, then jump and land perfectly on the horse again, and tumbled and spun until the audience was in a frenzy of appreciation.

One by one, the acts emerged, animals doing tricks, and jugglers doing impossible things, which Lionel seemed to like the best. Then again amid a puff of smoke, the *Amazing Aleksander, the Arial Genius*, was announced amid terrific fanfare. He was a lean, good-looking man, with reddish hair and a pointy face, dressed in a silver suit. He made flourishing bows in all directions, and then at a drum roll scaled the ladder in two or three movements, launched himself onto a bar hanging on two ropes from the high ceiling, and waited there for a moment.

"What's he going to do, Papa?"

"Trapeze, I warrant." said Mr. Marshall. There followed for Phoebe a fascinating show as she watched the *Amazing Aleksander* whizz through the air, catch the next bar with sure hands, and the next, becoming faster, and even turning and somersaulting between jumps. She stood on her feet and craned her neck to see him better. The audience gasped in ecstatic terror as he traversed the air above their very heads. Finally, he landed on his two feet in the middle of the ring, to tremendous applause and bowing over and over again, made an exit.

The band trumpeted again, and flashes of light followed darkness, as shadowy men ran about preparing the ring for the next act. Then the Ringmaster announced, with a great flourish:

"Ladies and Gentlemen, the *Incomparable Claretta!*" as a light shone upon a woman poised on a stand high above the ring, in front of her a thin rope that stretched across it to the other side. She stepped forward.

"It's tightrope walking," Mr. Marshall explained to Phoebe.

"I don't know if my heart can stand this," Mrs. Marshall exclaimed, her hand at her breast, while Lionel looked dumbstruck. An incredible silence from the watching public accompanied the *Incomparable Claretta* as she stepped forward on the rope. But she was sure and confident, almost breezy. In the middle of her walk, she stopped and whirled about, accomplishing a perfect landing back on the rope, in the midst of admiring vocalisations from all sides. She danced, twirled, and tumbled her way across to the other side.

The rest of the show was filled with the same thrills, another trapeze performance by *Amazing Aleksander*, this time with the *Incomparable Claretta*, who was announced this time as his sister. Together they flew through the air and were joined by even more acrobats who made gravity look like a fairytale.

"That was the best birthday I had, ever!" declared Phoebe, on their way home in the carriage through the dark streets. "I thought all the time that they were going to fall! What if they had, Papa? Would they have died? Maybe they have rubber bones. Yes, I think they must have rubber bones. I wonder if they ever fell on somebody's head. I want to be like the *Incomparable Claretta* when I grow up, I want to . . ."

"Enough, daughter, enough!" groaned her father, raising his hands in the air, but with good humour. "I don't know how you talk so much. Can you stay silent for just three minutes? I will bet you threepence you can't." He took out his watch and looked at it intently.

"Of course, I can, Papa! Was I not silent when *Amazing Aleksander* was flying over our heads? And when Claretta twirled into the air and landed on the rope? I know how to be quiet, Papa, don't I, Mamma? I'm quiet most of the time!"

"Shhh! Begins now!" said her father. Phoebe sat back and her eyes sparkled as she closed her lips in a tight line. She watched him with amusement as he watched his fob-watch. He looked up at her a few times and their eyes met in mutual affection and enjoyment of their little contest. It was a long, long three minutes, she swung her legs and nudged her brother, mouthing something with great expression, gesturing wildly with her hands, making him laugh, but not making a sound herself, until her father shut the cover on his watch with a click and put it back in his pocket.

"I did it, Papa! Now you can't ever say again I can't stay silent for three minutes! Threepence please!" She thrust out her hand for the coin, as he dug deep in his pocket and handed it over.

Mrs. Marshall smiled to herself. Most fathers and daughters did not have such a bond. She was glad for Phoebe, for though mother and daughter loved each other, they did not have that easy banter, that rapport, and she felt that her occupation as Matron afforded her little time to spend with her daughter. They seldom chatted. She was closer to Lionel, good-hearted, reliable, quiet Lionel, and he to her. His father tended to ignore him. She hoped that Lionel would not resent him for it. There was no jealousy of Phoebe on his part, however. Lionel was too generous of heart to feel that, and enjoyed his sister's capers.

Lionel began to talk of the animals; wondering if a tamer had ever been eaten. Phoebe joined in with her opinion.

"Yes, of course. I suppose when the tamers get old, they feed them to the animals."

"Children, your conversation is grisly," their mother reprimanded them, though she was amused in a shocked sort of way.

"I don't know why children think of the most gruesome scenarios," said her husband to her. "Is it peculiar to our offspring, Mother, or do they all do it?"

Everybody laughed. The children voiced some more rather imaginative scenes to shock their parents until their mother stopped them. Home at last, they drank milk and ate biscuits before they all went to bed.

"We should go out more, all of us together!" said Mrs. Marshall, in their room. "It's good for us, Richard."

"I very much enjoyed myself, Beryl. You looked very well tonight. You know it was your blue eyes that caught my fancy, the first time we met. They're very good eyes. Come closer, I want to see them better." He drew her near and wrapped her in his arms.

"Oh, Richard!" She snuggled to him and returned his kiss. Getting away from this place, even for a few hours, was enough to draw them closer.

Before they drifted to sleep, the name *Claretta* jumped into Beryl's head, as if it had been lurking there for some time.

CHAPTER SEVENTEEN

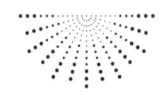

The supper was tasty, the wine sweet, and Dora was drifting dangerously toward the same error she had made more than eight years before.

She and Nancy had gone backstage after the show. Nancy had murmured her concerns, and Dora did not listen—she simply felt driven to try to see Aleksander. She had thought about him over the years, her heart yearned for him more than she had ever admitted to anybody, and their child was always in her heart.

She'd gotten such a turn when she'd seen her tonight! Little Phoebe, she wouldn't have known her, but for the Master and Matron. She was small but wiry, and her eyes were lively. She had the same features, the same eyes, as her father!

Why did she stay silent, all those years ago in the lying-in ward, when she could have gotten her back? These were her thoughts as she looked upward at Phoebe's father as he had, as effortlessly as seven years ago, swung himself with agility and grace from bar to bar. Tears had rolled down her cheeks. She looked about for the Marshalls when the

Big Top was lit again, but she could not see them. She longed to run and find them, run and get Phoebe and tell her that she had just seen *her father* perform in the ring, and that she could be *very, very* proud of him! She would never have done that of course, but she allowed herself the little dream.

Her heart burst to see Aleksander, and after the Show was over, she'd dragged Nancy, who questioned her wisdom but was nonetheless starstruck, to the back of the tent where she knew there was an entrance.

Suppose he was married? The thought made her pause for only a moment; she surged forward, inside the tent, and she saw him. *Would he welcome her?* Yes! He had changed into street clothes, for the troupe were about to go and eat, and he saw her and came forward, his face lit up with welcome.

Nancy hung back while the fond greetings were exchanged. He was not a tall man; he was not handsome, she thought, his features were too pointy; but he had a lean, muscular look and she could see why Dora was taken with him. He certainly seemed very taken with her, very happy to see her. Was this a true love story, like the ones she had heard of in magazines? Dora was in tears, he brushed them away with his hand.

He went away for a moment, and returned with his sister, the *Incomparable Claretta*. At this, Dora turned and introduced Nancy. Claretta did not have good English like her brother Aleksander.

She went with them, and the Troupe, to a restaurant in Dellmount Street, a place open late for actors and performers, of which there were many in this area at this time of night. Nancy and a dancer named Gisele, who had good English, chatted; while Dora and Aleksander retreated into a little space of their own, though they were at table with many others.

"I have thought about you all these years," said Aleksander. "and how you were, I was sure you had married by now. Why have you not been—what is the word—snapped up?"

Dora sipped from her glass.

"I didn't meet anybody I liked enough to marry," she said. "And you said you'd try to come back. I was sure you got married."

"*Nein*. What have you been doing? Are you still living with your father, selling fish?"

"Yes, still selling fish." She looked down at her hands, trying to hide them. They were working hands.

"I do wish I could stop travelling, and settle down," he said.

"If you did settle down—what would you do?"

"Teach acrobatics. Train children to become artists. But I would have to have some capital, to start off."

"Aleksander, you din't even write me after you left."

"My dear Dora, I cannot write in English. I know how to speak it from travelling with the Circus since I was a boy. Can you write?"

"No, not well. My name, and tha's all. I wish I 'ad an education."

"It is a big disadvantage not to have an education. I think, if I ever had children, I would insist on an education for them."

Dora's heart could bear no more.

"Aleksander, I have to speak with you alone. There is something I need to tell you."

There was a door leading to the outside, where there was a little garden and a bench. Together, they went there, and Dora, with many tears, told him about their child. He was very surprised, then angry, stalked away, shouted something in German. She sat and wept. Finally, he returned to her side.

"I understand why you did what you did," he said. "She will be well looked after as you say. And the other child? She lives in the workhouse?"

"Yes. I can't do anything about that. I stayed with her to give her a good, healthful start. Phoebe was here tonight," she said, somewhat impulsively. "Her parents—I mean the Marshalls—brought her. The name they gave 'er is Phoebe. I called our daughter Claretta, only they were mixed up, weren't they, so the wrong baby 'as the name Claretta now."

"Our child was here?" he stopped, intrigued and moved. "Phoebe, our child, Phoebe. I will meet her someday. *Ja*."

They returned to the Company hand in hand. Later, Dora threw caution to the winds once again, and she remained with Aleksander for two weeks, after which the circus left for Spain. She was utterly miserable when he left.

But he'd told her he'd come back. As to when, he could not say.

CHAPTER EIGHTEEN

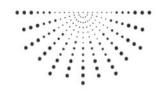

The summer passed, and Claretta was almost happy in her new surroundings. She made friends quickly, as Alice had lots of friends, and soon Mary, Josephine and Julia became hers also. She was not happy, however, with Mrs. Tate, who picked on her, constantly finding fault with everything she did, and reminding her she'd be *'prenticed out* and would have to know how to do this and that or her mistress would beat her. When Claretta one day, in a fit of boldness, told her that she had seven more years to learn everything, Mrs. Tate was so angry that she slapped her and dragged her to a cold, dark room in the cellar, where she remained all through supper-time with nothing to eat. When she was let out, Josephine had saved her a piece of her bread and slipped it to her without Miss Tate seeing. Claretta was almost afraid to eat it in case she was seen but managed it. She felt very grateful to Josephine, a kind girl whose mother was living in the Women's Wing, and when she visited often gave her little treats she'd somehow acquired, and which she shared with them.

Claretta wished she had a mother. She wondered what it was like to call somebody "Mamma." She tried it out once or twice to see how it felt. She said the word "Mamma" when there was nobody about, in the yard, in a corner. But the word went into thin air. She had no mamma. She did not remember the woman named Dora who Martha had told her was her mother. But Martha did not like to talk about Dora, that she knew, so she had stopped asking her.

CHAPTER NINETEEN

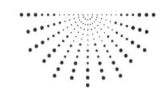

Phoebe looked out enviously at the Girls' Yard. She was supposed to practice writing her name. Mamma and Papa were at the weekly Board Meeting, Lionel was gone to stay with a schoolfriend for a week, and Annie, who was supposed to supervise her, was having trouble with the range today, so she had forgotten Phoebe. The girl had left the table and gone to the Solarium, which gave a view of all the yards. She saw the girls her own age with a skipping rope. Two girls were holding the rope, one at each end, for a queue of girls who one by one went into the rope and skipped, leaving it to allow the next one in. The open window received their chant as they skipped.

A Sailor went to sea, sea, sea

To see what he could see, see, see

But all that he could see, see, see

Was the bottom of the deep blue sea, sea, sea!

Out went the skipper, in with the next without even a pause, and the chant began again.

It wasn't fair! She had no friends to play with or skip with, and she was not allowed to play with the paupers! She was supposed to be friends with the Braddish and the Goulding girls when her mother took her to visit them, but that was only once a week, and she didn't like them anyway, they played with dolls all the time and didn't want to run around as much as she did. She felt different.

She could not bear it any longer; she'd go and play with the pauper girls. They could not refuse to allow her into the skipping game; she was the Master's daughter. She slipped down the stairs and along the corridor that would bring her to their building, but found the door locked.

But Phoebe was a determined child, and a locked door was not going to stop her. She went to their private garden, which had a wall, the other side of which was the Girls' Yard. She climbed the old oak without any trouble, until she could see over the wall. She hoped that Annie wouldn't look out the window.

One of the girls in the yard spotted her, and nudged another, and soon there was a group of girls staring at Miss Marshall in the tree. Far from frightening her, it emboldened her. There was a branch sticking out toward the wall, she'd go as far as she could on that, and it was only a short drop to the wall. But quickly! Before any grown-up person saw her!

She sprung herself from the branch and landed on her feet on the wide wall, only taking a moment to regain her balance, hearing gasps from below her. She gauged the distance to the ground. It was too high to jump—she knew that with the instinct of a cat. She was pleased to see that she had the attention of the entire yard. She began to walk—but it was impossible for her to walk normally—she hopped, extending her inactive leg over the edge of the wall as far as she could. She took off her shoes, they were making her feet heavy. She threw them into the garden.

The wall was much wider than her narrow foot. It adjoined the corner of the Girls' Building, and this was her destination, and from there she could make her way to the ground via a pipe. In the meantime, she was enjoying the adulation from the girls below. The skipping had stopped, and every eye was upon her. Her destination was forgotten. Since she had been to the circus, she'd been practicing the movements of the *Incomparable Claretta* in her room, pretending a single floorboard under her foot was a tightrope, being very strict about keeping inside the edges as she hopped and leaped her way to the other end of the room. The wall was much wider than a floorboard, and she was utterly confident. She began to leap and jump with abandon; she was the *Incomparable Claretta* and revelled in her triumph.

CHAPTER TWENTY

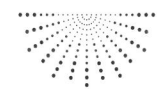

Dr. Pearse had to attend the Board Meetings, but he found them extremely boring, and the quibbling over expenses endless. Matron was haggling for new curtains for the lying-in room, and he felt that she expected him to defend her request to the Board, but as it was not a question of medicines, he kept silent, pretending not to hear, looking out the window that looked on the yards.

"Gracious me," he exclaimed suddenly. "Mr. Marshall, is that your daughter on that wall?"

The Master hastily got up, followed by the Matron, and then the entire Board of Guardians congregated around the window. They were all in time to see little Miss Marshall execute a perfect cartwheel just below their view. A slow, careful, but perfect cartwheel. Then another, a little faster. And another, faster still.

Matron fainted. Mr. Marshall was ashen. "Phoebe!" he said, hardly daring to speak. He shook.

"Now do not be nervous, Marshall," said someone, seeing his utter terror. "She will be all right, but this needs to be halted now."

The youngest and most agile of the Board, who happened to be the clerk, nipped down the stairs with the intention of rescuing her himself, if that is what it would take, and it occurred to him to wonder if the rescue should go in the Minutes.

But by now, other people, nearer to the scene, were drawing near and shouting: *"Get down!" "Don't move!" "Shut up all of you! She'll lose her nerve!" "A Ladder! Quick!" "Get a fireman!"*

There was Annie screaming from a window, Mrs. Tate shouting at the girls, who were only guilty of enjoying themselves immensely; a pauper attendant leaning halfway out a nearby window beckoning Miss Marshall to the safety of the building. There was chaos.

But the girls were thrilled to pieces. What an unexpected treat! Excitement washed over them like a wave. Already more than one of them had attempted a cartwheel, with varying success. Someone began to clap, and they all began, with a helpless, furious Mrs. Tate moving among them to get them to stop.

Seeing Mrs. Tate spoiling everything, Phoebe regretfully decided it was time to retreat, but not before she remembered to give a few flourishing bows, which she executed in all directions, to the girls below, then to the enraged Annie, and lastly to the attendant with her arms out the window, and she performed all three with tremendous aplomb. The girls clapped harder and shrieked their appreciation. Her performance was partly visible to those in some of the other yards, so they took up the applause. Those who could not see decided to clap as well, as something good seemed to have taken place.

It was her next move that old Mr. Browne joked later ushered in his dotage. She sprang herself from the wall toward the tree, caught a branch with one hand, reached for another with the other hand, and spinning around and around, swung from branch to branch until she was of a distance where she could safely drop to the ground and retrieve her shoes.

She happened then to look up to the Octagon to see several pairs of stern eyes looking out at her from the Boardroom, and her heart sank. Annie was now before her, her face like thunder, and hauled her in.

"You're trouble, you are! But who is to be surprised at that? Your mother was a good-for-nothing!"

There was chaos when she reached the Master's apartments.

Her mother shrieked at her, she could have been killed, and the whole world had seen her bloomers; her father did not speak but looked very solemn and pale, walking up and down the room. Annie threw her glances of fury and banged cups and plates about.

She was banished to her room and her toys taken away, her rag dolls Annabelle and Algernon, her toy animals, her hoop and her top.

She heard her parents quarrel. Her father was saying it was not her fault. Dear Papa! She loved him more than she loved anybody in the world. Papa said it was *Annie's* neglect. Her mother said that the fault lay with him—he encouraged her in these daring schemes.

"My little tumbler," he said to her later, taking her hand, "Your poor mother and I got the fright of our lives. You must never, ever do that again."

"I'm sorry, Papa," she mournfully said.

"Of course, you are." He kissed her goodnight. After he had gotten over the initial shock, he'd begun to feel quite proud of her. She knew no fear. If only she'd been born a boy, she could be a great general, dispatched on dangerous missions to far-flung corners of the Empire! He was sure that the Board of Guardians had been silently very impressed with her skill. He did not think it would result in any reprimand for him, though Kitson had managed to remind him once again as to why a Master and Matron should not have any children living with them.

It was time for their night rounds; he in the Male Wing and she in the Female, but tonight Beryl declined to leave Phoebe until he returned.

"They are supposed to be done at ten o'clock in summer," he pointed out. "Ask Annie to keep an ear open for Phoebe."

"About Annie. She's given notice. She says she can't be responsible anymore for Phoebe. Her antics frighten her. Today just about finished her off."

Matron wrote her a good reference and Annie departed two weeks later.

"I'm sorry Annie's gone away," Phoebe said. "Mamma, did you tell her to go away because she thought you were a good-for-nothing?"

Her mother was astounded.

"Annie left of her own accord, and you must be mistaken, Phoebe. I'm sure she never thought such a thing about me!"

"She did, Mamma, when she brought me in from the garden the day I got up on the wall. She was very angry and she said, *'Your mother was a good-for-nothing.'*"

Mrs. Marshall was silent and very perplexed. She was still sure that Phoebe had misunderstood.

CHAPTER TWENTY-ONE

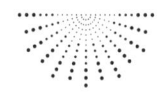

Summer passed uneventfully in the Girls' Wing. Their days were a strict routine, up at six, breakfast at seven, then work. Darning, sewing, scrubbing, washing, mangling, ironing. Cleaning and more cleaning. They took exercise twice a day in their yard. Mrs. Tate was still nasty to Claretta and a few other girls. Claretta was afraid of having to go to the punishment room again. She was afraid in there. She had heard there were ghosts of girls who had been sent there and forgotten about, so they died there. She obeyed Mrs. Tate without question, and every day, her heart was in her mouth as she went about inspecting her work. If Mrs. Tate found fault, she had to begin all over again and miss the recreation in the yard with the other girls.

In September, to her relief, school began again. Miss Penworth was a good teacher, and she flourished under her guidance, and she was very happy for the three hours she spent there. Upon the advice of Dr. Pearse, the class was also taken on a walk to a wood weekly. There, they played in great delight among the trees, hide and seek or swinging from the lower branches, or picking flowers, and had a wonderful time until it was time to return. Mrs. Tate always berated them because their pinafores got grubby and anybody who tore one had to go without supper.

They saw no more of Miss Phoebe. Never did she appear at the window, and never did she get up on the wall for a repeat performance. Martha, on a visit, told Claretta that she had heard that she had been sent away to school.

CHAPTER TWENTY-TWO

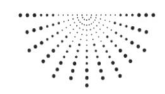

"You're in the family way again, aren't you?" said Mr. Davis, disgusted, as he threw a catch of fresh sole into the barrel. Dora said nothing. "I thought the last time would teach you a lesson. Wasn't it enough to have to spend two years in the workhouse, slavin' at pickin' oakum? Now here we are again. What are my respectable customers going to say? Mrs. Greenway and Mrs. Hitchens. When they see you, they'll never come again."

"I'm sorry, Papa."

"Who is it this time?"

"It's the same father, Papa."

"Why the devil won't 'e marry you, that father? If I could get my 'ands on 'im I'd make 'im. He must be an awful sort of fellow to leave you like that. Twice."

"He's with the circus! He travels all over! He's *The Amazing Aleksander*!"

"He's the *Abominable Aleksander*. You know you 'ave to go away again, Dora. Get back, get back there—look who's a-comin', good morning Mrs. Greenway, fancy some fresh 'erring today? Or fresh Dover Sole just in, brought in not 'alf an hour ago."

Dora slipped away, dodging between the stalls and stands that made up Blackbell Market. She pulled her shawl over her stomach to hide her shame.

It was going to be the Workhouse for her again.

The Board had a record of her admission over seven years ago. She stood before them, humiliated that she was again in need of charity, with the same mistake she'd made before. They were severe in their attitude also.

"You have a child here already," Mr. Kitson said to her sternly. "Her upbringing is a burden on the Ratepayers. Now here you are again, and this child, I suppose, will burden us also. You have never come back to see your child, have you?"

"No," she whispered unhappily.

She could see that the men thought little of her. She was a fallen woman and a bad mother.

"Do you have any hope of relief from the baby's father?" asked Braddish.

She shook her head.

"Is he married?" asked Mr. Holborne.

"No, he is not."

"Does he have employment?" This from Mr. Goulding.

"Yes, he works with a circus. He travels a lot."

The Guardians seemed rather intrigued. Perhaps boyhood memories of the circus arrested their train of thought.

"Pray what does he do in the circus?" asked Mr. Browne, in a voice that suddenly seemed to have woken up.

"An acrobat. His stage name is *The Amazing Aleksander*."

Silence greeted this. She thought some of them were rather curious and would like to ask more. Maybe some of them had seen him. Mr. Kitson cleared his throat.

"We shall accede to your request for asylum here, Miss Davis. I need not explain the rules to you, you know them."

"Yes, sir. Thank you, sir."

"You may go straight to the Receiving Ward."

"Thank you, sir." She turned to go, relieved that the interview was over at last. But they had not finished. Mr. Braddish was speaking.

"Miss Davis, a moment please. Just one more question. This man, the father of your second child, is he the father also of your first child?"

It was a very personal question and she resented it; but they were entitled to ask whatever they pleased.

"Yes, he is."

CHAPTER TWENTY-THREE

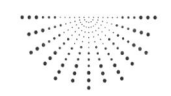

Matron knew immediately who Dora Davis was when she heard her name. She was the mother of Claretta, who she always remembered was born on the same day as Phoebe. She went to see her without delay, made her as comfortable as she could without seeming to welcome her back, drew up a diet suitable for an expectant mother, and told her that Claretta was growing up to be a sweet child, and reports from the school were very favourable.

"I'm 'appy for her." said Dora in a monotonous tone. Matron sighed to herself. She had encountered this before, this maternal indifference. She supposed that when a mother was unable to care for her child and had given her up to the care of the parish, that she put the child out of her mind to elude her own heartache. She had never come back to see her child, and that showed an attitude that Matron regretted.

"How is your own daughter, Matron?" Dora called after her as she was leaving.

"She is very well, away at school."

"Away at school." Dora hardly bothered to hide her disappointment at not being able to see her. Still, there was Christmas and she'd be home then, she supposed. Matron was perplexed at her rejoinder. An odd woman, Dora Davis.

The months wore on, and on the Monday after Easter, Alexander Davis was born. Matron delivered the baby, who cried right away, and handed him to the attendant, who made ready to bathe him.

"Matron, the baby 'as a birthmark," said Kate. "Look there, on 'is hip."

Matron examined it. It was the same *café au lait* birthmark that Phoebe had. Light brown, smooth. The same place too, and the same shape. *Identical.*

A dreadful thought entered her head about the day seven years ago. She dismissed the idea, but it persisted for the evening and into the following day. What if—? Was it possible that—? It nagged her like a pebble in her shoe. She forced herself to complete the *what if* so that she could think with reason. She drove herself to contemplate the possibility that the unthinkable had happened, that somehow, the infants had become switched. No, no—but the birthmark —*identical*—

Phoebe was her daughter, no matter what her origins; she would always be her daughter, always be Miss Marshall. But if her own child was growing up a pauper, here in this workhouse, with the stigma of illegitimacy when there was none, and a life of servitude in her future—that would be intolerable! She could not live with any peace, if that was the case.

She had to get information before she mentioned anything of the matter to Richard, for she knew what his reaction would be.

Unknown to Beryl, one or two of the Board had their own suspicions. Years ago, rumours had surfaced, and they had laughed at them. They had come from the inmates and were not to be taken seriously. It was just the sort of hysteria that poor and ignorant people were prone to. They had taken steps to quell the rumours, for they should never reach the Master and Matron's ears. Dr. Pearse had been helpful in this undertaking, as had Mrs. Bateman. All the same, the rumour refused to die. It had happened, some claimed, when the pauper baby (the name was forgotten) was taken to the Octagon for examination, because the doctor was in a hurry to the Races (this was well-known). He also was half-drunk (unknown to the doctor, every adult inmate—and some of the children, from the memory of alcohol-sodden relatives outside—knew he drank).

Dr. Pearse mixed up the babies.

CHAPTER TWENTY-FOUR

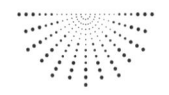

Matron hoped she was wrong. Hoped that her suspicions would be laid to rest. She sought out Mrs. Bateman and asked her to visit her in her office.

"I have a particular reason for asking you to tell me your memories of the day my daughter was born." she said. "Particularly with regard to her medical examination and that of the pauper's child Claretta Davis."

Mrs. Bateman looked down at her hands. She took a deep breath.

"It was seven years ago, Matron, but I will do my best. Both babies were examined in your parlour by Doctor Pearse."

Matron went pale. She exclaimed her dismay in a plea to Heaven.

"Go on, go on!" she said, her head in her hands.

Mrs. Bateman related the events of that day to her, including how she had instructed Doctor Pearse that the pauper baby was on the left side as you look into the basket.

How she had had to go and see to Lionel, and how when she returned, both babies were in the basket. She had dressed them both and returned the pauper baby to her mother.

"Do you remember seeing the birthmark on Phoebe's hip?"

"No. And Doctor did not see it. He only examined their top half."

"He did see it, because when I asked him about it, he seemed to know about it . . . he asked for another look at it . . ." her voice ebbed—"*another* look. Devious man!"

"If he put the baby back on the wrong side, then we have the Davis baby and our child is growing up in the workhouse," she stated slowly. "I don't know how we are going to ever find out the truth."

Miss Bateman's heart raced. Would she tell her? She swallowed hard.

"What is it, Mrs. Bateman?"

"That evening, on my night round, Dora Davis mentioned to me that she thought she had the wrong baby back."

Matron sat up straight, her hands folded on her table, her knuckles white.

"Mrs. Bateman! And you did nothing about it!" she shrieked.

"It was too late to do anything there and then. It had been a hectic day, and everything was shut up for the night, including your apartments. First thing in the morning, I went back, and asked her about it—she told me that she had been mistaken—she had her own baby back, she said, and she was certain of it."

Matron stared at her. "You should have acted that very night," she said sternly. Mrs. Bateman nodded. "I should. I know I should. It's haunted me, particularly since—"

"Since what?"

"Since Miss Phoebe doesn't resemble either of you, and the Davis child . . ." she did not finish the sentence.

"Leave me," commanded Matron, her face the picture of agitation.

That evening, Matron had an agonising wait for her husband to come in from the Men's Wing where he was overseeing a delivery of quarried stone for the Tramp Ward's work. At last, she heard his step in the hallway. She made him a cup of tea.

She related all to him, and he was utterly incensed.

"What you are saying is utter nonsense!" he said with an angry voice. "What has taken hold of you, woman? To say that Dr. Pearse confused our child with a pauper child! It's beyond belief! I will hear no more of this, do you hear me? I will never hear this again. You are to take your enquiries no farther. Are you completely out of your wits? Cease and desist! Phoebe is our daughter. There cannot be any doubt on that score." He drank all the tea in one go and pushed the teacup away.

He was shaking with anger. He took up the newspaper and held it in front of his face, blocking her view. She knew he was not reading the newspaper. He was still shaking with anger and his thoughts were of what she had told him.

You are to take your enquiries no farther.

The newspaper was lowered suddenly to show a red, angry face.

"Remind me, what is the name of this child born the same day as our Phoebe?"

"Claretta Davis."

"You are never to mention her name to me again. If you do, I shall petition the Board to have her removed to another establishment."

"Richard!"

"This discussion has ended." The newspaper blocked her from his sight again.

CHAPTER TWENTY-FIVE

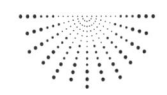

Mr. Braddish, Mr. Goulding and Mr. Kitson were friends, as were their wives. They ate dinner with each other often. The ladies always retired to the drawing room after dessert while the men drank port and smoked cigars at the dining room table. They often used this opportunity to share tidbits of information, or opinions, about the Union Workhouses, topics which were not suitable for meetings. They discussed contentious issues and made pacts and deals against other members. Sometimes the wine at dinner and the port after dessert were responsible for a certain rashness.

"A rather odd fact," said Mr. Braddish. "About that pauper woman, Dora Davis."

"Pauper woman!" Kitson was surprised. They never talked of the inmates unless a colourful character had unwittingly provided an amusing anecdote.

"Her child—her older child, who is eight years old now, was born on the same day as Mrs. Marshall's."

"Was she? And that is of interest? Why?" asked Goulding.

"Because here is the curious thing. You heard Davis say, when we readmitted her recently, that the father of her children is a circus acrobat."

"What of it?" Kitson asked.

Braddish leaned back in his chair and inhaled his cigar slowly.

"Do you remember one day at a meeting, the commotion caused by Miss Phoebe Marshall's antics on top of an eight-foot wall?"

"Why of course. I shall never forget it. Wonderful cartwheels too, quite dazzling, though I should never allow my daughter to make a display like that, if she could do a cartwheel, which I doubt," said Mr. Goulding.

"Well, gentlemen, have you any thoughts?" Braddish asked after a pause.

Goulding frowned. Kitson shook his head. Braddish spoke again.

"Two children born the same day, one is the daughter of an acrobat—she showed an impressive talent, did she not? And she never had a lesson in her life, I daresay."

"Good gracious. You aren't saying that—" Kitson looked astonished beyond belief.

"I am not saying anything. I am just speculating."

"Well you'd better not speculate to anybody else, man; there would be the devil of an uproar. What are you going to do?" asked Goulding.

"I plan to ask Dr. Pearse about it. Whether he knows if the infants were ever brought together in the early days."

"And—if you find that an error had—or may have—occurred?"

"We'll have to bring it to the Board. And the magistrate...."

"—who is related to Dr. Pearse."

"And Dr. Pearse will deny all, when you ask."

"Let us know, man. Let us know."

Mr. Goulding and Mr. Kitson were not in suspense for very long. At their next dinner, at Mr. Kitson's home, Mr. Braddish reported that he had approached Dr. Pearse in the very same manner as he had his gentlemen friends, in a speculative way, and that Dr. Pearse had said that there was no way that he knew of, that the children could have been confused.

"And do you believe him?" asked Mr. Goulding.

"Not at all. But we must leave the matter there."

"Can't you ask the mother? The Davis woman?" Kitson asked.

"I've no doubt the inmates think I'm a heartless man, from the harsh way I question them, but you know we cannot make any inmate feel welcome when they come to us. Nevertheless, I do feel for them sometimes. Among the list of deceased persons this last week is Dora Davis. Cause of Death—puerperal fever."

"Oh, that is unfortunate. God have mercy. And the child?" asked Goulding.

"In good health and sent out the country to be suckled."

"They have it hard, don't they? The paupers. Not sure it is their own fault, though some say so." Goulding said. "It seems to me, we could do more—"

"Let's join the ladies, shall we?" Kitson got up from the table.

CHAPTER TWENTY-SIX

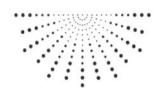

Martha's weekly visits to Claretta continued. It was a time she treasured. Martha was not sure what her reaction would be to the news that her "mother" had died. She was surprised that Claretta cried.

"Am I not as good as any Mamma to you, Claretta?"

"Oh, yes, Auntie Martha!" Claretta was afraid to appear ungrateful. She didn't remember her mother and she couldn't understand why she was sad, but she had hoped in her heart that her mother would come back and take her away to live in a house, away from Mrs. Tate, whose latest cruelty was to threaten to send her to Canada, a place Claretta had never heard of, but she supposed it was outside London. She did not know what her mother looked like, but she thought she must be very pretty, and smiled a great deal and perhaps she was like Mrs. Winter, Thomas and Alice's mother, who was affectionate and always had Alice on her lap when she visited. Mrs. Winter always had a kind word for her too.

But now, her mother was dead and so was her dream.

Martha had to leave her soon after that and went back to the Nursery. She was again seized with a pain that seemed to tear her stomach apart. It was happening more often. She'd have to ask to see Dr. Pearse. What if she were seriously ill? What would become of Claretta?

CHAPTER TWENTY-SEVEN

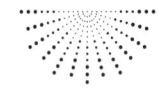

Jane Eldred arrived one day in response to a summons from her sister Beryl. She'd been very alarmed at the tone of her letter. Beryl had hinted at a family crisis that she could not resolve, and that she was scarcely objective at this point, was at her wit's end, and needed her to come and help her to put things into perspective.

Seated at her table over a pot of Twinings tea, Beryl poured out all. Jane silently blamed herself for not speaking out when the children were much younger, but that could not be helped now, and it would not be helpful to mention it.

"I cannot take it any further," Beryl said. "You see my position? I feel, in my heart, that Claretta belongs with us. Every time I see her, my heart jumps with something like— recognition. It's hard to explain! I think she's mine. My heart tells me."

"Dora Davis died; Dr. Pearse will probably deny any switch could have happened; Mrs. Bateman has, I assume, told you everything she knew? I have one thought," said Jane slowly.

"Was there anybody else present at the birth that day, or perhaps in the lying-in ward with Miss Davis?"

"I don't remember. It was so long ago. But we do keep records! Oh! Wait I do remember now, a woman named Martha Ballard. Dora asked me particularly to send her to work in the Nursery, because she had lost all her children, and had taken a liking to Claretta."

"Is she still here?"

"Yes, she is. She's in the Infirmary now with severe abdominal pain. Dr. Pearse thinks she has stomach cancer."

"Oh, poor woman. Perhaps she noticed something—or Dora confided in her—"

"I can't approach her. It would cause trouble between Richard and me, not a good beginning for any investigation."

Jane was tapping her fingers on the table.

"I have it."

"What?"

"You cannot know my plan. You can plead innocent!"

"Oh Jane, I knew my own sister would be of help! Would you like to see Claretta? I think I shall go and take her to see Martha."

"Of course."

"Let us go now, then. And I want to know what you think of Claretta."

They arrived at the Girls' Wing to the sounds of an angry voice and a child crying.

"I'll have you sent to Canada! Do you know where that is? It's as far away as the moon! Nobody lives there! Only wild animals! That's where we send useless orphans!"

"Mrs. Tate, what is this about?" asked Matron in a severe voice.

Mrs. Tate was taken aback to see Matron at this time of day. She had a visitor with her, too. She tried to make the best of it.

"Claretta Davis has a lazy streak, Matron. I told her to clean the windows, and she left spots!"

"I heard you threaten her with Canada, Mrs. Tate."

"Only a joke, Matron."

"Eight-year-old girls do not clean windows, Mrs. Tate. You may go to your room now. I will make a decision about you later."

"Oh Matron, I did not mean—it was only a joke—the girls find it quite funny—"

"Claretta is not finding it funny, Mrs. Tate. Go now, if you please."

Mrs. Tate threw her head in the air in a defiant gesture and walked away.

"It's all right, Claretta. We will never, ever send you to Canada. Now dry your tears. I'll take you over to see Martha, would you like that? Come along, then. Martha is ill, she looks a bit under the weather, but you mustn't tell her so. All right?"

Beryl took the child's hand on the way over to see Martha, on her way giving instructions to an attendant to fetch Miss Penworth to look after the girls.

While Beryl had been reprimanding Mrs. Tate, her sister had been eyeing the child. The dark hair, the set of the features, the large blue eyes—she was an Eldred.

CHAPTER TWENTY-EIGHT

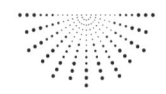

"Auntie Martha!" cried Claretta as she ran to the woman lying in the white bed and flung her arms about her.

Even in the poor light of the Infirmary, Jane thought that the woman looked alarmingly ill. Her skin was yellow-white; her cheekbones marked, creating great hollows. But she smiled to see Claretta. Many of her teeth were missing.

Matron walked about the ward, greeting the patients, inspecting the nurses' stations and the general state of things. She left Claretta with Martha for about twenty minutes before calling her to come away.

Jane's mind had been busy. When Claretta had left Martha's bedside, she had approached it.

"The little girl is very attached to you, Miss Ballard," she began.

"Yes, that she is, Miss." Tears brimmed in Martha's eyes.

"She calls you Auntie."

"That she does, Miss. A blessing to me she is, too."

"I'm Jane Eldred. Do you know that Matron is my sister? I think I would love Claretta to call me Auntie as well. Can you help me at all?"

Martha looked at her intently and nodded.

"I'm not long for this world," she said. "Anything I can do for the child, I will. I wish I could write, I would put it in writing, nuffink's any good if it's not in writing, Miss."

"I will write for you, if you tell me what to write. I'll come back tomorrow with pen and paper. You can whisper it to me, so nobody else hears."

"The sooner the better, Miss."

Claretta went back to the Girls' Wing and ate her supper. She was both frightened and happy about today. Frightened that Mrs. Tate would take revenge for Matron being angry with her; happy that Matron had been kind to her, and that she had held her hand! Happy too that she had seen Auntie Martha. That had been a surprise! But Auntie Martha looked different in the Infirmary than she looked when she visited her. Very different. She looked very ill.

CHAPTER TWENTY-NINE

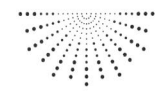

After breakfast the following morning Jane, unknown to Beryl, armed herself with paper and pen and returned to the Female Infirmary to take Martha's letter. But she stopped abruptly at the door of the ward. Martha's bed had another patient in it.

"Where did you move Martha Ballard to?" she asked the pauper attendant in the corridor, who was tying up soiled linen in a large canvas bag.

"Why, to the dead-'ouse, of course," was the reply.

There was a chair by the wall, and Jane sank onto it. All hope drained from her.

"What happened?" she asked, after a moment.

"She took bad sudden last night. Right afore I go off to supper, Doctor Pearse comes, and she calls 'im over, and says something to 'im—about she was goin' ter write a letter or something, she seemed agitated about it—then I went to my supper, an' when I come back, she takes bad and dies around midnight."

Jane digested this, bewildered.

"Was Dr. Pearse still 'ere? Here?" She corrected herself hastily.

"We called 'im in this mornin', 'e had to certify her before we could take her to dead-'ouse, din't 'e?"

"So, he was here in the evening, and knew she was to write a letter, possibly incriminating to him, and she died soon after?" Jane murmured aloud, but mostly to herself, as the attendant moved off, dragging the linen bag after her.

A form materialized before her. She looked up. She was startled to see Dr. Pearse. He looked old, and tired.

"She wished to write a letter, yes." Dr. Pearse said. "And—she did write it, she dictated it to me, and here it is." He fished in his pocket and with shaking hands, drew out a folded sheet of paper, putting it into hers. "She feared she would not last the night. And she was correct. I think this is the letter you are expecting. Read it, Miss Eldred. I have written my own letter also, about the matter in question. It is time."

Jane unfolded the sheet and read the letter. It contained the information that Miss Dora Davis had confided to her that she knew the baby she got back was not her own, because her own baby had a birthmark on her hip, and this baby did not, and that she intended to say nothing because she wanted her daughter to have a better life than she had.

CHAPTER THIRTY

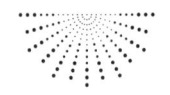

Jane said nothing to Beryl, beyond saying that she knew Martha had died. Matron, of course, had been apprised of that depressing fact early in the day. Jane burned to share her secret but could not. Her brother-in-law must never know this letter had been instigated by her. Hopefully Dr. Pearse would leave her name out of it, also; he'd have no reason to mention it.

She waited. Beryl was very sad about Claretta's bereavement. She had told her, and Claretta had been distraught, flinging herself on the floor, crying hysterically. She had instructed Alice Winter to stay by her side. At least Mrs. Tate was not in the Girls' Wing anymore. Matron did not have the authority to dismiss her; she could report her to the Board, but she had the power to move her and move her she did, to the worst place she could think of, the Wash-house, and she made it clear she did not have the authority to punish anybody without referring the matter to her first.

CHAPTER THIRTY-ONE

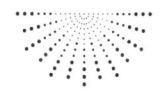

Jane Eldred did not have to wait long. Dr. Pearse had presented the Board of Guardians with his and Martha Ballard's letters, and they immediately called a meeting, at which Master and Matron were to be present. Along with his letter, Dr. Pearse had offered his resignation. He was not present.

Richard Marshall was flabbergasted, shocked, and disbelieving.

"This pauper woman," he retorted, "saw an opportunity to secure this child she was fond of with a future. She acted on rumours, and since the girls were born on the same day, it stood a great chance of success. Can't you see how deceitful these people are? If you had to deal with them on a daily basis as I do, you'd recognise this as the cunning trick it is."

"And Dr. Pearse's testimony?"

"It means nothing! He admits to nothing except a possibility that the children were confused!"

"We have made further enquiries, Mr. Marshall. Dr. Pearse was on his way to the races and had already imbibed alcohol when he visited your apartments. We confronted him with this allegation, and he confirmed it."

"I still do not believe it," exploded Mr. Marshall. "Phoebe is my daughter! Nothing will change!"

"Mr. Marshall, it must change. We have determined that the girl we knew up to now as Claretta Davis is no longer entitled to receive Union Relief. As for Miss Phoebe—her fate will be up to you to decide, you and your heart and your conscience."

"Forgive me gentlemen, but I still cannot accept—" Marshall threw his hands in the air. "I'm telling you that Phoebe is my daughter!"

"We understand your difficulty, Mr. Marshall, but perhaps this might help you," put in Mr. Goulding. "When Miss Davis was admitted for the birth of her second child, we questioned whether the father was the same as her first, and she said yes. What's more, she told us that he was an acrobat in a visiting circus, *The Amazing Aleksander* no less. I believe you took your family to see the circus in which he and his sister *The Incomparable Claretta* performed. Do you need further evidence that an unfortunate mistake occurred?"

Mr. Marshall was now robbed of speech. In front of his mind passed the scene in this very Boardroom, where he had been summoned to the window to see Phoebe execute a series of perfect cartwheels on top of the eight-foot wall. She was not just emulating Aleksander and Claretta.

She was one of them.

The truth became clear then. It all fit together now. He seemed to sink back into himself.

"When can we take custody of our daughter?" Matron asked with eagerness.

"This very day, Mrs. Marshall." was the reply. "We have already begun the process."

CHAPTER THIRTY-TWO

They went back to their apartments, dazed. Their servant, Jenny, put on the kettle to brew a pot of tea. Mr. Marshall was silent.

"Shall we go and fetch her within the hour?" asked his wife.

He made no reply. His eyes were staring straight ahead.

"You look as if you have been hit by a train, Richard," his wife said. "Pray, what are your thoughts?" But he simply shook his head.

"I don't want any tea," he said, suddenly getting up and leaving the apartments. They heard his footsteps fade away.

"Oh God in Heaven," Mrs. Marshall prayed, her head in her hands. "Please come to our assistance!"

"We trust Him, no matter what." Jane said with firmness. They were both silent until the tea came in.

Mr. Marshall left the workhouse, not acknowledging Bateman at the gate, and walked smartly along until he came to his brother Daniel's cottage.

"Richard," was his greeting. "Come in. You look ill. Brandy?"

He poured him a shot. Marshall drank it down in one go and placed the glass on the table with a thud.

"You've had a shock, Richard," said Daniel. "Tell me."

Richard related his story.

"To find out that the child you loved as your own is not yours, and that the child you cared nothing about is yours—I don't know what to think about it. Why did God do this to us?"

"He did not. But God can make good come out of bad. He does it all the time, turns the table on the devil."

"Daniel, you cannot be calling this *good?*"

"You have your rightful daughter back, and you love another child who would not be otherwise loved, is not that good?"

Mr. Marshall was silent. His expression showed his thoughts very well.

"You have a choice before you, Richard. You can continue to close your heart to one or even both—or you can open your heart. Choose to love, or choose to reject."

"I would never reject Phoebe!" he cried out, getting up and walking about the room. What he was actually saying hit him with force. He was talking about a pauper child! A child born out of wedlock! A nobody in the world, from what he had often called *'the dregs of society.'* And he loved that child! Peace trickled into his heart and mind. That was an easy choice.

"But what of the other?" he said, turning around suddenly. "I don't know! How can I take a child raised with paupers into my house? I don't love that child. Will I, ever?"

"Rich, love is often a decision on our part. *'If today ye hear His voice, harden not your heart.'*"

He left Daniel soon after. He walked straight through the workhouse gate and to the school. He opened the door of the girls' classroom. Forty pairs of eyes looked at him. None of them pleased to see him. He noted that.

"Claretta Davis?" he said. He saw heads turn towards one little dark-haired girl, and the teacher told her to stand up, which she did, with eyes wide.

"Come with me, Claretta." he said. He held out his hand.

She hesitated, her eyes even wider, turning to the teacher.

"Well go on, Claretta," said Miss Penworth. She had no idea what the Master wanted, but he was the Master.

Claretta walked with dread toward the Master. He led the way outside the door and shut it. They were alone in the corridor.

"Please don't send me to Canada." she whispered.

"Canada? Gracious, child, no. Don't be afraid. Do you know who I am?"

She nodded. Beryl's blue eyes looked up at him.

"And do you know Matron?" She nodded.

"Matron is your Mamma, Claretta. And I'm your Papa. I'm taking you now to your Mamma. Come with me." He held out his hand, and after hesitating briefly, she took it.

CHAPTER THIRTY-THREE

Beryl was overjoyed to see her husband return with Claretta.

"Are you really my Mamma?" the child asked incredulously. "I thought my Mamma died."

They hadn't prepared themselves for questions.

"I'm your Mamma now," said Beryl. Time enough for explanations, when she was older. But what would they tell Phoebe? At least the girls were still young enough to accept what was told to them. "And you have a sister named Phoebe."

"The girl on the wall." said Claretta. She looked like a waif standing there, in her regulation frock and pinafore.

I need to get her out of those workhouse clothes, thought Beryl, *Phoebe's might fit her, though she's a little bigger. Does she fully understand that this is where she is to live now?*

She took her back to the workhouse, and all the protocols were observed in discharging her. Dressed in Phoebe's clothes, and clutching Ruth, her only possession, she accompanied Matron back to her Quarters.

CHAPTER THIRTY-FOUR

"Phoebe Marshall, can you go to the Headmistress's Office please?"

Phoebe wondered which of her escapades had got her into trouble now. Last week, she'd tried to climb a drainpipe to rescue a cat on the roof, which did not need rescuing at all, but Miss Merrick had seen her. Or maybe it was yesterday, when she'd mounted the donkey who'd wandered into the front garden. Neddy threw her off. Her bruises had to be explained to Nurse.

She was surprised and delighted to see her father in the Head's office.

"You're leaving us for the rest of the term, Phoebe." said the Headmistress, with a certain relief.

"Why, Papa?"

"Pack your things, I'll explain on the way home."

On the walk to the train, carrying her suitcase, he said: "You have a new sister."

Phoebe was astounded and delighted. She'd always wanted a sister to play with! And it was not a baby, but a girl her own age called Claretta. *Claretta!* Her favourite name in all the world! She loved her already.

CHAPTER THIRTY-FIVE

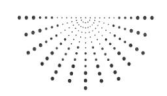

"We've been sisters for seven years now," Phoebe said one sunny day when the girls were wandering about the poppy-filled meadow near their home, the sprawling old country workhouse named Lowick. "Do you remember Blackbell?"

"Not very much," said her sister. "I remember being afraid of Mrs. Tate, and being lonely, wishing I had a mother. And knowing I would be *'prenticed out*. I remember my friends very well, especially Alice Winter. I hope Alice has a good place with a kind mistress. I remember her brother too, and her mother. And Aunt Martha of course. Without her, I think I'd have been terribly unhappy."

"I don't remember much either before you came, except I got into awful trouble for turning cartwheels on a wall once."

Phoebe immediately turned a series of cartwheels in the poppy field.

"Stop, Phoebe!" her sister giggled. "We're very near the road! What if anybody's watching?"

"Oh, if only I were a boy, I could turn cartwheels all day long and nobody would mind."

"I remember the day you got up on the wall, and how you bowed to us after the performance, and that Mrs. Tate got angry with us for clapping."

"And I remember all the Guardians' eyes looking out the window when I got down," giggled Phoebe.

"Mamma and Papa must have thought a sister would calm you down and maybe that's why they adopted me. And they felt sorry for me because I'd lost Martha."

"We aren't real twins, I know, even though we were born the same day. Do you think there's a secret, Clara? A secret about us?"

"I don't think so," Clara said. Some years ago she'd announced she wanted to be called Clara, preferring it to Claretta, and her mother and father had agreed readily.

"I think there is. And that's why we moved from Blackbell. Because everybody there knew it."

"It doesn't matter if there is, does it?" Clara wondered little about her past. She remembered how when she came to live with her papa and mamma, it had been very different. She'd been awed by everything; been very comfortable in her soft bed, had lots of different foods to eat, but had been fretful and lonely too—missing her friends and crying sometimes for Martha. Her papa would not allow her to go back and see her friends. She'd been quite afraid of him for a while, even though he it was who had brought her to his home. When Phoebe came home from school, she'd told her: *"Oh don't be afraid of Papa! Be like me, I'm not afraid of him!"* Clara had looked to Phoebe for guidance on everything, and if Phoebe wasn't afraid of "The Master," she wasn't going to be afraid either, though it had taken her some time to call him *Papa*. Lionel was a kind big brother. Her mother and father had forgotten to tell her that she would not now be apprenticed out, and she asked Lionel. He'd said: "No, Claretta, of course not. You're not going to be a servant *now*."

When her new Mamma had found out she longed to see shops they had made a special excursion to the city. That had been a very memorable day—her first time seeing bustling streets, bright lights, beautiful big buildings, and the River Thames. And what she had heard was true—you could get anything in a shop if you had the money! Mamma had allowed her to choose three ribbons for her hair. She'd chosen red, blue and yellow.

She smiled suddenly.

"Why are you laughing?" asked Phoebe.

"I remember Mamma took away Ruth. She said she had fleas. So, she gave me your doll instead, because I was in floods of tears."

"Yes, but she knew I wouldn't mind. If she had given you Tiger, I would have been angry, but I never cared for Annabel."

"Heyday! Phoebe! Clara!" called the voice of a young man from the road.

"It's Lewis!" Phoebe waved to the young man who was passing by. He was the grown-up son of the rector Mr. Epworth. A friendly, smiling fellow, he'd been their friend from the time they had arrived, and never minded the difference in their ages.

"Where are you going?" called Clara.

"To Aunt Fran's! I have to take scones to her from my mother!" he grimaced at the foolish task, then brightened. "If you come with me, she'll give you some to eat!"

"No, but thanks. We have to go home!"

"Did you hear," he shouted then, "About the foreigner who came to the village yesterday?"

The workhouse was situated two miles from the town of Sudford, and the village of Lowick was between. All it boasted was a tavern and a grocer's shop. A foreigner in the village was news indeed, because there were few local attractions to draw tourists, English or otherwise, either to town or village.

The girls ran swiftly to the hedge separating them.

"No we didn't hear of anybody! Tell us! Who is he?"

"He's German! He's lodging in the Swann. Nobody knows why he's here."

"Maybe he's a cousin of the Royal Family!" joked Phoebe.

"He wouldn't put up at the Swann, Phoebe!" grinned Lewis. "Well I had better get on. Are you sure you don't want to come with me?" he asked in a pleading voice.

"We do want to come with you very much, but we can't." said Phoebe. "You know Papa's a stickler for time."

They walked back to the workhouse. Their home there was larger than the one in Blackbell, and they occupied a good-sized parlour and three bedrooms. The fourth bedroom had been turned into a dining room. Mrs. Marshall had insisted on it so that they could eat Sunday dinner together and at other times also, celebrate birthdays at suppertime, even if the food had to be brought over from the kitchens.

It was the girls' birthday today. They were fifteen years old. Phoebe was small-boned, but very strong. Her red-gold hair shone in sunlight, her eyes reflected the good cheer she always had in her heart, and more often than her mother liked, glimmers of mischief. She'd retained the elfin look she'd had as a small child, but now it would be said that her face was heart-shaped. Clara's face was rounder, her eyes a forget-me-not blue, her creamy complexion framed by abundant chestnut hair. Both girls were keen to put their hair up for now they considered themselves young ladies, and they planned to do it this evening before they presented themselves for supper, to surprise their parents. When they realised that they might not have as much time as they thought, they quickly ran through the poppies.

CHAPTER THIRTY-SIX

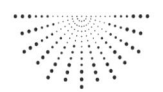

Their father looked at them with alarm.

"Girls, what have you done?"

"We're fifteen now, Papa! Clara did my hair, and I did hers." Phoebe twirled about, to show the elaborate way Clara had arranged her hair on top of her head. "It makes me taller!" she said happily.

Papa did not like change. When they had first come to Lowick, he had taken quite some time to settle into his new job; hadn't liked the Guardians; and thought the workhouse had been very ill-run before. The years had mellowed him somewhat; Daniel, a frequent visitor, had had something to do with that. The Master had become gentler with the destitute under his care.

He'd remembered that love is often a decision, and decided to love Clara, until one day he realised that this love had grown roots and was now strong and blooming, though Phoebe still held first place in his heart.

Mrs. Marshall upon arrival at Lowick had had to correct many slovenly practices to give the paupers their Rights as laid down in the Poor Law. She was supported in this by the Rev. Epworth, Lewis's father and another Guardian, who was pleased to see an ally. She and Richard were nearly of one heart in everything now and she was very happy, if fatigued from work. Right or wrong, she credited Clara's coming to live with them with this change in Richard.

"It's very nice, girls." Mrs. Marshall examined each hairdo. She was a little wary that Clara might look more like her with her hair up now. But she had become grey and wore spectacles, so she hoped nobody would see a resemblance.

They had agonised over whether to tell the girls the truth about what had happened all those years ago, but they had not asked. Phoebe assumed she was born to them; Clara thought she was adopted. Everyone thought they were twins. At age twelve or so Phoebe had wondered why she did not look like her parents and brother, but her father had told her that he had cousins in Scotland that looked very like her. She accepted it completely and it was never mentioned again.

Lionel, at seventeen, was a studious, reliable lad. Still quiet and good humoured, he had finished school and hoped to become a schoolteacher at Sudford. Lionel had learned the secret when he had finished school. As the eldest, he would act *in loco parentis* if anything happened to the old couple, so they wanted him to know. As Lionel had grown, Richard had become closer to him, and the more he slowed down, the more he looked to him.

They heard a trolley in the hallway.

"Quick," said their mother. "Open the door!"

They did as asked and sat down without delay to roast beef and mashed potatoes, which was not so very cold. After eating, they had birthday cake and oranges.

CHAPTER THIRTY-SEVEN

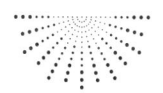

Aleksander Brandt looked out the window of this small pension, in the village of Lowick, pondering what he should do next. He'd returned to England to begin a School of Gymnastics. His purpose in choosing England was Dora.

He'd visited her father, the fishmonger. He replayed the visit in his mind, recalling his consternation and grief in finding out that not only was Dora gone from the world, but that he had a second child, a boy, the fishmonger said. He hadn't thought much of the *fischhändler*. A selfish man. But then the fishmonger had not thought much of him, who had got his daughter into trouble not once, but twice.

If only he hadn't married his cousin Gertrud, but he had been seventeen, and she twenty-seven. They had been forced to marry. There had never been love between them. They had never had children. When Aleksander had come to England, he'd fallen in love with Dora. He'd lied to Dora about not being married, but he did not feel married, and bitterly resented the union. He'd returned seven years later and blissfully renewed the love affair. He'd had no idea another child had resulted.

He had injured his shoulder badly in Buda, and it had never fully recovered. His career had ended at thirty years of age. Gertrud had died last year. He was free. He ran a school in Posen, but England was on his mind, so he persuaded his sister Claretta to come with him.

He had only a little money; his earnings as a boy had gone back to his father. He had enough to rent a few rooms, and one of them would be a large room which he could fit up for students of acrobatics. That was how he would keep his family.

But Dora was dead. Their daughter had grown up in a family and it would be unfair to take her away from the only mother she knew. But he wanted so much to see her. He looked at her name written on a piece of paper. In the case of the boy, he would take custody of the boy.

He would take a walk tomorrow to the place where he knew she lived. For now, he went downstairs and ordered a *bier*. The landlady put a mess of mutton and potatoes in front of him, and he had to ask for bread with it. The landlady sniffed. When the bread came it was plunked down in front of him as if it were a great inconvenience.

CHAPTER THIRTY-EIGHT

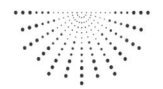

The girls had great freedom during the summer because their mother was busy. Clara liked to go to the workhouse every now and then to help; she never forgot she had been one of them once, and she wanted to help in the nursery and talk to people. It was becoming more acceptable to bring the inmates treats now, in the form of books, magazines, and other simple entertainments. Her parents were agreed that it might be good for her to train as a Nightingale Nurse; they were much in demand now.

Today, there was a new attraction for the girls. The German. They often walked to Lowick, and they just might see the interesting foreigner if they went there today.

"But we can't go into the tavern." Clara objected.

"I know that! There's a wall opposite beside the stream. We can sit on that and pretend to look at the water. What do you think a German looks like, Clara? Will he have a feather in his hat?"

They walked along the quiet road that led to Lowick Village, chattering. They passed a terrace of cottages they knew well, greeted an old woman sitting in a doorway, and crossed a little bridge where an angler, Mr. Kitchen, told them they were disturbing the fish with their noise. It was ever so with him.

Turning a corner, they saw a man walk toward them. He was a stranger with red hair, and a little beard. He walked smartly, swinging his cane. *The German?* They fell silent as he approached, pretending not to examine him, but taking in the good suit of clothing, the shiny shoes and beaver hat.

He lifted his hat and stopped.

"Excuse me young Misses, am I on the right road for Lowick Workhouse?" he asked, with a click of his heels and a slight bow. He had a foreign accent! It was the German!

"Lowick Workhouse!" exclaimed Clara.

"Straight on ahead, Mr. emm?" Said Phoebe, always the quicker of the two.

He did not take the hint and declare his name.

"Actually, we live there, and we can walk with you and show you," she said brightly, all thought of the village forgotten.

"Oh, but were you not—?"

"We were just walking aimlessly," said Clara, silently congratulating Phoebe for her quick thinking. They turned around.

The man would have no option but to walk with them now!

"You're not from around here, are you?" asked Phoebe.

"No, indeed. I am from Prussia. But I live in London now. You have heard of Prussia, I'm sure."

"Prussia is in Germany!" Phoebe said with triumph.

"We live in Lowick," said Clara. "Actually, our father is Master of the workhouse there. I suppose it is he you're going to see?"

He gave them a quick look, and it seemed to the girls that he became a little short of breath.

"Maybe we should rest a while," said Clara, kindly.

"A good idea, Fraulein."

They sat on a wall, but the German did not sit, he walked before them, looking at both girls with interest.

"Father is very busy today," said Phoebe. "I was wondering if you had an appointment?"

"*Nein*. I do not wish to see your father. I am merely enquiring. Do you know if there is a man named Otto Kessler in the workhouse? He was the servant of an old friend, who, when he heard I would be in this locality, asked me to check."

"We don't know the names of the inmates," Clara said. "I do know some of the women. But I think we'd know if there was an Otto Kessler, because it's so unusual. We know there's a man named Juan Gomez, for instance, from Spain."

He nodded.

"There is probably not much point in going there then," he said, looking at the sky, before looking at them suddenly. "I am Herr Aleksander Brandt. Who do I have the pleasure of talking to?"

"We're the Marshall sisters. I'm Phoebe and this is Clara."

"It is a pleasure to see you." He held out his hand and Phoebe took it first. He looked from one to the other and back again.

"Now, which one of you is the older?" he asked.

119

"We're twins!" Phoebe supplied the information.

"Twins! You are not so alike for twins."

"We're not identical." Clara said.

"Born on the same day, though, you have to share your birthday with your sister every year, *ja?*"

"We don't mind. In fact, yesterday was our birthday." Phoebe offered.

"Yesterday! Now let me see, you were—seventeen perhaps?"

"No sir! Only fifteen!" Phoebe said, flattered.

Clara thought the stranger was a little too forward, fishing perhaps. She made as if to go. He took the hint.

"Goodbye again, then, Phoebe and Claretta."

"*Claretta!*"

"Forgive me. Clara." He flushed and bowed, again clicking his heels.

He took off the way he had come, leaving the girls mystified.

"How odd that was," said Phoebe as they walked along slowly. "I've heard the names *Aleksander and Claretta* before, used together. Where? Oh, where?"

They walked in silence for a few minutes before Phoebe came to a sudden halt.

"I know! They were acrobats from the circus we went to many years ago! I'd never really forgotten them! I used to copy Claretta's act at home. Could it possibly be him, Clara?"

"No, it's your imagination, Phoebe!"

But Phoebe turned smartly around.

"I'm not letting him go just like that, I'm going to follow him!"

"Don't be silly, Phoebe!"

But she had to accompany her sister. They followed him at a distance, without chattering. He didn't walk smartly anymore, his head was bent to his chest. At one point he stopped, took something from his pocket, and threw it into the hedgerow. It seemed to be an angry gesture. Phoebe gripped her sister's arm.

"It was around here," whispered Phoebe a few minutes later. "Let's look for it!"

"Here's a crumpled piece of paper," said Clara. She opened it, frowned and shook her head.

"How very odd this is, Phoebe!"

Phoebe snatched it.

Tochter geboren 6 juni 1868 Mutter Dora

"I don't understand this language. But it looks like our birthdate, Clara. What can it mean? Who is Dora?"

A memory returned to Clara—her mother's name. The mother she never remembered.

"Phoebe," she said with astonishment, "If Dora was my mother's name, could that be my father? Does *Mutter* mean Mother? And I was *Claretta* then!"

CHAPTER THIRTY-NINE

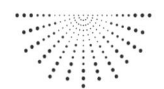

"What is the matter with you, Clara?" Matron asked quietly at breakfast the next morning in the staff dining room. They always spoke in muted tones as the staff would lap up everything they could overhear and gossip about it. "You look as if you haven't slept a wink."

"She didn't." said Phoebe.

"Are you ill?" asked Mr. Marshall. "You're pale as a ghost."

"She thinks she met her natural father yesterday," whispered Phoebe.

The parents, and Lionel, fixed their eyes on both girls. There was shocked silence for a moment or two.

"It doesn't matter whether I have or not," said Clara bravely. "I don't remember my mother, and you've been parents to me more than they have. I don't want to think about it, and I don't want to talk about it, if you all don't mind." She buttered her bread and closed her mouth firmly.

Nobody said anything. Phoebe thought her parents looked distressed and uncomfortable. Even Lionel looked upset.

At the Tavern, Aleksander Brandt was eating a breakfast of bread and sausage and drinking *kaffee*, which he deemed hardly worthy of the name. He ran his mind over the events of the day before. It was well he had met the two young ladies on his way to the workhouse, because he had no idea of what he would do when he was to have arrived there.

He felt both happy and heartbroken, if such a state was possible in unison. Happy that his daughter Phoebe was looking in health, a bright, engaging young lady, at ease with herself and with the world. And so like the Brandts! He was heartbroken that he had missed her childhood and had not had the opportunity of seeing her grow up. He wondered if she had any of the Brandt talent. He wondered many other things. Most of all he bitterly resented that he had not been free to marry Dora. It was wrong of him to have taken advantage of her; he had asked God to forgive him. He had lied to her, giving her hope. A hope that could never have been.

The Marshalls knew of the mix-up and had taken their own daughter back. And they had not abandoned Dora's child. They must be good people.

Satisfied that he had seen his eldest child and that she was well, he now must turn himself to the task of finding his other child. Back to Blackbell! His son was now seven years old. He was in a home somewhere, in a workhouse, or a "cottage home" or maybe an orphanage. He hoped that it would not be complicated. He not only wanted to do this for the child himself, but for Dora also.

He'd visited her grave. It was a small, poor affair with a simple marker, a small metal cross. He'd got flowers and put them there. He'd wept there a great deal.

CHAPTER FORTY

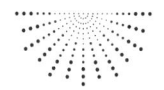

"Our first real Ball!" cried Phoebe, waltzing around the room in a flouncy gown. "It will put the Assembly Rooms in the shade. Will anybody important ask us to dance, do you think? You'll fill your card without delay, with your large eyes and long eyelashes. As for me, I'll be lucky if I get one or two, from Lewis Epworth."

"Lewis likes you," said Clara. "You and he always have a good laugh together."

"He's very agreeable, but ordinary," complained Phoebe. "I want to meet a rich, dashing stranger. We'll be nineteen this year, Clara! It's time for us to fall in love!"

"Are you ready, girls?" Mamma came in to inspect them. "You're showing too much shoulder, Phoebe. Clara, what's that red stuff on your mouth?"

"Just a tiny bit of rouge, Mamma."

"My daughters will not paint themselves! Rub it off."

Clara complied with a sigh, while Phoebe made a show of trying to hoist her sleeves higher.

"You look nice, Mamma," said Clara. "Thank you for talking Papa around."

"Your papa is very protective of you both. I shall sit and chat with the neighbours while you enjoy yourselves with the other young people. Behave nicely and don't let us down."

The Twelfth Night Ball was being given by Sir Nigel Lucas for his daughter who was turning eighteen. Everybody from miles around had been invited. His son, Tristam, was home from Oxford. The Marshalls were not gentry; the invitation was an unexpected surprise; they had never been inside the walls of Lucas Manor. They knew the young people only to see them riding by. But Sir Lucas was a Guardian so he was well known to Master and Matron.

Phoebe looked enchanting in emerald satin. She exuded colour, life and energy while her sister, in shell pink, had a demure, but no less appealing look. They'd worked on the gowns for weeks, staying up late stitching and trimming and helping each other with fittings.

Pheobe's dance card filled up quickly—the first two with Lewis, then Tristam Lucas for the next two, then a youth of only about sixteen, which was a waste of a dance, Tristam again for two, another two with Lewis, and Tristam, Tristam and Tristam. Everybody noticed that he was paying her a great deal of attention. Clara had less luck, two with Lewis, one with Tristam no doubt on account of her being his favourite's sister, and the rest with various swains from around the area, some known to her, some introduced that very evening, but nobody memorable. She sat a few out and watched everybody.

Phoebe was smitten. On the way home in the doctor's carriage, borrowed for the occasion, she spoke of Tristam. "He's going to call on me on Wednesday, Mamma."

At home, Mrs. Marshall called Clara aside.

"Try to talk her out of this romance," she urged. "Tristam will have to marry well. We are not good enough for the Lucases. Please promise me you'll try, Clara. I don't want her to get hurt."

Clara felt like a wet blanket when she broached the subject later. Phoebe was indignant. How dare Clara try to tell her what to do! And Mamma put her up to it! Well, she had news for them. Tristam had told her that his grandfather had been a merchant. He could not possibly object to her. Clara retreated, feeling ashamed. She told her mother, who sighed.

"Mamma, surely it's not all that important," Clara said. Her mother made no reply.

Tristam came on Wednesday as promised, riding through snow to see Phoebe. He came the following Saturday and Sunday, and they went for walks, Clara following a little way behind. Over the next several weeks into the spring, he came twice a week.

"I love Tristam, Clara." Phoebe said dreamily one evening. "I think he loves me too! Do you think that this time next year, I might be Mrs. Lucas?"

CHAPTER FORTY-ONE

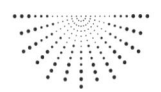

"You asked for me, Father?" Tristam entered his father's study.

"Yes, sit down, chap." His father looked solemn and fiddled with his pipe. "It's about this girl you like, the Marshall girl."

He waited until his son was seated to begin.

"You have heard me mention a good friend I have in Town named Benjamin Kitson."

"I have heard you mention his name, yes. What's he got to do with—"

"He's a Guardian for Blackbell Union. A long time ago, when he approached me to ask if I could take Mr. and Mrs. Marshall into our employ, he told me something I have never told to anybody, not even to your mother, and you must swear to me you will not disclose this to anybody either. It is a very sad and strange story."

He began to relate it, and young Mr. Lucas was revolted at what was revealed to him. He thanked his father profusely for saving him from a most unpropitious attachment.

CHAPTER FORTY-TWO

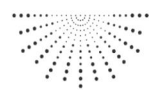

"Oh, why is he not coming?" cried Phoebe. Tristam had said he would come over to see her this evening and he was late. The early March wind blew chilly, and there were spatters of rain. Night was closing in. She looked out the blurred window for him, in vain.

Their parents napped on and off in their chairs as was their habit, then got up and went on their evening rounds. Night was upon them. Everybody went to bed.

The following day, the porter came with the post. There was a letter for Phoebe. Clara watched her read it, her face crumpling with every line, her mouth trembling. She sank into an armchair and burst into tears, burying her face in her arms.

Clara took up the letter from her lap. It was from Tristam. His father was sending him away and he did not know when he would be back. He wished her well with her life.

"His meaning is very clear, there can be no doubt about what he means! What can have happened?" she sobbed.

Clara knew that no words of hers would comfort her. Phoebe went to bed and Clara sent a message to her mother to come over straightaway after her morning round.

CHAPTER FORTY-THREE

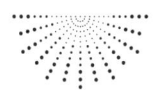

It was nighttime; the storm still raged outside. Phoebe appeared to sleep at last, laudanum had lulled her into a calmer state. Clara could hear her parents and Lionel arguing in the parlour.

She threw a shawl around her shoulders and left the bedroom. If it was about Phoebe, there was no reason she could not join in. Their voices were raised, so she didn't hear Phoebe awaken and call her name. She opened the parlour door and stood on the threshold. They did not see her.

"The knowledge would devastate her!" her father was saying. "She was just unlucky. Kitson must have told Lucas. Lucas told his son. They couldn't take it, the stain of illegitimacy, the pauper mother. I was against them going to the Lucases. You should have refused that invitation, Mother."

"Don't be ridiculous, Richard, how was I to know she'd fall in love?"

"Tell the girls," urged Lionel then. "Because this may happen again. And Clara has a right to know she was born into our family."

She exclaimed aloud, drawing attention to herself. She could not believe her ears.

"The cat's out of the bag now," said her father. He lifted his hands in a helpless gesture.

"What happened? Mamma? What does Lionel mean?" asked Clara, perching herself on the arm of her mother's chair. Her mother took her hand and pressed it.

"You're ours, Clara. You were born a Marshall. There was a dreadful mix-up the day you were born. Both you and Phoebe were examined at the same time in the Master's Quarters. You went back to the pauper woman, Dora Davis, and Phoebe stayed with us. We didn't find out for years and years. Please forgive us for not telling you."

"Whatever do you mean?" Phoebe's small frame stood in the doorway now, her voice quavering. She trembled all over and leaned against the door. "I'm the pauper child?"

CHAPTER FORTY-FOUR

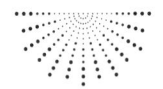

"She isn't speaking to any of us. She's impossible." Richard said to Daniel as he planed a piece of timber. "If she does speak, it's to quarrel. She thinks we're all to blame for the circumstances of her birth; instead of being grateful to her mother and me. Clara has far more reason to be angry with us, but she isn't. The reason we didn't tell Clara she was born to us, was to spare Phoebe. She had more to lose. Clara doesn't seem to be bitter about her years spent in the workhouse."

"She doesn't remember most of it though," Daniel pointed out. "How much do you remember of your life before you were eight years old?"

"Very little. But Clara has, for over ten years, thought she was adopted, and now she finds out she isn't. If I were Clara, I think I would have something to be angry about. But Phoebe is the angry one."

"Does Phoebe know who her father is?"

"Yes. They met him, you know, he came here some years ago. They tumbled to who he was, but thought he was Clara's father. Now she knows he was her father and she's forgotten everything I ever did for her. She's an ungrateful pauper brat."

"That remark is beneath you, Richard. I hope you haven't said that to Phoebe."

"No, of course not, nor will I. When we're angry, our thoughts fly off in all directions. What was that saying—about turning thoughts into words?"

"*'Guard your thoughts—your thoughts become your words.'* How is Beryl?"

"Very hurt. We're both exhausted. This could well take a few years off our lives."

Daniel stopped his work.

"What exactly is Phoebe blaming you for? Not being told?"

"Yes, that. And—we told her that she has a brother and she is angry that we did not take him in after he was weaned. How could we? We did not feel obliged to do so. We were not supposed to even have children as Master and Matron, and we had three."

CHAPTER FORTY-FIVE

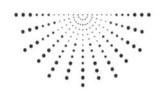

"Why aren't you infuriated?" asked Phoebe, lounging on the chair. "You aren't normal, Clara. *Claretta*." she added with sarcasm. "I hate my mother Dora," she went on. "She must have been a very stupid person."

"You're infuriated enough for both of us," said Clara, mending a stocking. "Why don't you take some of the mending and help me?" She pushed the basket toward her. It was a lovely May morning, and Clara wanted to finish up so that she could go out and enjoy the trees in their early summer glory.

"No. Why should I? I shouldn't even be here, should I? I should be selling fish or blacking a grate somewhere."

"I hardly recognise you anymore!" Clara said to her in a raised, exasperated voice. She put down her work and went over to the workhouse. Phoebe was becoming very difficult to live with. Clara was spending more and more time in the Nursery, in the Female Infirmary helping the nurses, or in the Girls' Wing being kind to the little ones. Helping there always took her mind off trouble. She thought again of the Nightingale School for Nurses in London. But she did not want to go away yet—she'd just found her real parents! The thought brought her joy. She thought to herself that it was not a giant leap from knowing she was their natural daughter from where she was before, their adopted girl. Nobody in the family had ever made her feel an outsider, Lionel and Phoebe had taken her to their hearts. She understood the dilemma her parents had been in. Still, they must have known it would be revealed someday. But she could not be angry with them. They had righted the wrong done to her as best they could. If she had to be angry with anybody, it would have to be Dr. Pearse and Dora. Especially Dora. She should have done the right thing when she knew there had been a mix-up. At least this explained why Dora had never come to see her. That had hurt.

Yes, she was angry with Dora. But if only Phoebe could calm herself and count her blessings!

Phoebe ate her supper in silence and went to bed early. Clara took a drink of milk before she turned in for the night. She slept deeply until morning. When she awoke, she saw that Phoebe's bed was empty, and her clothes gone. There was a note.

Dear Mamma, Papa, Lionel, and Clara

I have been horrid to you all. Please forgive me. I need to get away, don't try to follow me. I have to make my own life now. I love you and thank you from the bottom of my heart for all you did for me. I have to find out where I came from. All my LOVE, Phoebe.

CHAPTER FORTY-SIX

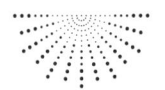

Phoebe had left before dawn. She had hitched a ride on a passing cart to take her to Sudford, and from there boarded a train for London.

She knew what she was going to do in London. She'd find her grandfather, or if he was dead, someone who knew her mother. Her unfortunate, foolish mother. That'd be a lead to her father. "*I live in London now,*" he'd said. She wanted to find her brother. It burned her that her brother was in a workhouse. Why couldn't her parents have taken him, too? They did not even remember his Christian name! Her anger with them ran very deep.

Cheap lodgings in London were easily found in Whitechapel. She set out for Blackbell Workhouse for an address for her mother. Bateman was still there, and his wife, and she chatted with them for a while, telling them the truth of why she was there. She got her mother's last address from the Master. She was disappointed to find that her grandfather had died, and in that workhouse too. Disconsolate, she walked around the streets for a bit.

She'd already found a way that would lead her to her father. Perhaps circus people all knew each other. She made her way to Victoria Park, hoping to find a circus there, and was fortunate. One person asked another, and another, and soon she learned that her father had opened a Gymnasium in Hackney.

It had been much easier than she'd thought! Soon, she was standing outside the gymnasium. The door was open, so she let herself in. She heard voices and thuds—a class perhaps? She pushed open a door and recognised the man she'd met in Lowick, supervising a class of half a dozen boys as they tumbled on floor mats and climbed ropes.

He turned and saw her, and not seeming to know who she was at first—a sister of one of the boys perhaps—then went on with his work. Then upon a closer look, he recognised her and came over. He was overjoyed to see her, and that *she* had found *him!* She wept. He called one of the boys over to him.

"Your brother Alex," he said, "He's training to be an acrobat, like me. I found him, three years ago."

She embraced her brother, who looked astonished that he had a sister. He had green eyes and fair hair, and she wondered if he took after Dora.

"I can't believe I'm seeing you," she said. "My own real brother!"

"My sister Claretta is upstairs," Aleksander said. "She keeps house for me and trains the young girls also. I will take you up there."

She was to meet *The Incomparable Claretta*! Her aunt! And leading the way in front, was *The Amazing Aleksander* she had watched with awe all those years ago in the Big Top. Her father! Was she dreaming?

As she ascended the creaking stairs, Phoebe could hardly believe her luck. She hoped they'd invite her to stay—they would, wouldn't they?

The Marshalls need never be a part of her life again.

CHAPTER FORTY-SEVEN

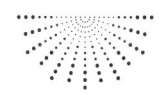

Phoebe had expected an ecstatic welcome from Aunt Claretta when it was explained to her who she was; but instead, the petite, blonde-haired woman looked just surprised, saying nothing. Was she unwelcome, then? Her heart sank with disappointment. Her father said something in German, and they conversed in that foreign language for a few moments.

"Will you stay here?" asked Aleksander.

"I would love to, if it wouldn't be any trouble." said Phoebe. Did she not belong here?

"You will share Claretta's room."

She went back to her lodgings and collected her small suitcase and came back, elation in her heart. She was beginning a new life, and tonight she would tell them about her ambition to become an acrobat and ask them when she could begin to train with them.

Claretta led the way into her room in a rather unwilling way, and Phoebe felt she did not want to share it. It was a shambles—dresses, costumes, hats, shifts, jewellery, knick-knacks, cosmetics, framed photos of her on the tightrope, shoes, everywhere. And it was small, with only one bed, and that unmade. How could they share this place? A small wardrobe was stuffed with clothes.

The flat was very small. There was just one kitchen-parlour, and two bedrooms leading off it. It was rented of course, and the exercise room downstairs also. A servant lived in an attic room. Phoebe did not think much of Sonja's skills or her manner. She did not speak English.

She wondered if flats in London were just terribly expensive, or whether the family was not doing well here.

Supper was a sort of dumpling with sauce, which Phoebe did not take to, but wanting to fit in with them, she ate it bravely, and ate the bread offered without butter.

Her brother was a sweet boy, but he spoke like the workhouse children, badly, like Clara had. Phoebe resolved to teach him how to speak better English. She had coached Clara.

Lowick seemed a million miles away already.

Claretta spoke to her brother in German,

"My sister wants to know what work you will do." Her father said.

"I want to train as an acrobat."

Claretta smothered a laugh. Phoebe blushed and felt deeply hurt.

"I'm very good," she defended herself. "When I was eight years old, I climbed a high wall and did cartwheels on top of it, a narrow wall." She remembered that she had been emulating *The Incomparable Claretta*, her idol, the woman who was now laughing at her.

Aleksander spoke sharply to Claretta. She stopped and said something.

"She is sorry for laughing, but you see, you are too old to begin."

"Too old!"

"Yes, even little Alex was too old at eight, to achieve the level of perfection that one needs to be a first-class acrobat. He will have to work very, very hard. *Ja,* my young son?" He thumped his shoulder.

"Yes, Papa. But I'm not afraid," he said stoutly. "I want to be an *Arial Genius* like you!"

Her age was something she had not thought of.

"Talent is not enough?" she asked, afraid that Claretta would laugh again.

"No. Not enough at all. Not for a professional level. That is years and years of hard work."

"What age should you begin training?" she asked.

"We began soon after we could walk. Our playtimes were spent on ropes."

What a bitter disappointment this was! Only a few weeks ago, she hadn't cared about becoming an athlete, she wanted to be Mrs. Tristam Lucas. But when she had gotten it into her head, she felt she belonged with the Brandts and with their lives.

"I am sorry," he said. "But if you have talent, and I'm sure you do, you can train for something not so demanding. Claretta works in Fawcett Music Hall on ropes and trapeze. Many music halls have specialty acts, and if you could achieve a certain level, perhaps you might be able to work in the business. You would need to train. It will be very hard work, you know? Claretta has a class in the morning, you can join it."

CHAPTER FORTY-EIGHT

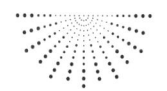

She passed an uncomfortable night wedged between Claretta and the wall. Claretta had most of the pillow. The aroma of coffee drifted in soon after light, and Sonja came in and poured water in the ewer for washing.

Phoebe climbed out the end of the bed, washed and got dressed and went to the kitchen. Her father handed her a cup of black coffee. There was a plate of fresh rolls on the table. She took one, and reached for another, to find her hand stopped by him.

"Strict diet," he said. "If you are serious about training."

"I am," she said, stoutly.

Claretta put her head out the door, holding the basin of water, calling Sonja. She shouted something in German. Phoebe felt embarrassed. She should have thought of emptying the basin.

Her little brother was up soon after, and his father began to school him in German at the breakfast table, and Phoebe felt left out.

"We're giving England a try for another year," said her father. "And if it does not work well, we are going home. So far, it is only so-so."

"Oh." Phoebe felt as if she were on the edges of their lives. But of course, she was, she reminded herself, she had only come to them yesterday! Why did she expect to be embraced and accepted immediately? She did not know them, and they did not know her! What if they went back to Prussia, and she did not go? She would lose them all over again.

Her training session was not pleasant. Firstly, she was the oldest in a class of children and Claretta shouted at her as much as she shouted at the younger ones. She felt humiliated. But she wanted to learn—what else could she do? She'd shed the Marshalls, she would have to make her own way, wouldn't she? Or, could Aleksander keep her? Why not? He was her father, wasn't he? He hadn't had to keep her all through her childhood, surely he would be generous now!

She had to get some proper *culottes* like the other girls had. She'd worn Claretta's. She'd have to ask him for money.

After lunch, slices of pickled ham with some bitter cabbage, which she disliked, she approached her father.

"I'm running out of money, Father" she said to him casually. "I'm going to need an allowance."

"An allowance!" he said, in surprise. "I was going to ask you how you were going to pay for your keep and your lessons."

"You're my father!" she said to him, stubbornly.

"And you're a grown woman! Claretta was earning long before she was your age! No, no allowance! You bring in your own money, Phoebe. Hasn't your father given you any?"

This stung. She backed away. Her eyes filled with tears. He hastened to her side and put a hand on her shoulder.

"I am sorry," he said. "I am, of course, your father. I am clumsy. It is difficult. We grew up not knowing each other. We are strangers. Let us go out this afternoon. I'll take you to your mother's grave."

CHAPTER FORTY-NINE

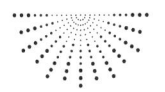

He bought flowers at a stall outside the cemetery, two bouquets, and gave her one. Together they went to Blackbell Cemetery and soon were standing by the silent grassy mound with the metal cross.

Phoebe did not feel anything. That worried her. On the other hand, Aleksander did. He knelt and crossed himself and prayed quietly, his brown eyes with a faraway, wistful look. She knelt by his side. The only emotion she felt was loneliness. This was the first time she'd stopped to think since she'd left Lowick and it rushed into her head that she missed the Papa and Mama she'd always known, and Clara and Lionel. Very, very much. Then there was *Tristam*. It was too much. She burst into tears.

Aleksander was very kind. He put his arm about her. They got up then and went away. She felt a little relieved. Phoebe felt she had left something there at the grave. Maybe her sorrows. She resolved to try harder at her new life. On the way back she told Aleksander about Tristam. He was very kind, fatherly, told her everybody gets a broken heart. He had! And her mother! He began to tell her about Dora. She listened intently. She didn't like how he'd lied to her, though. He went down in her estimation. But it was so unfair that he had been forced to marry his cousin. Was a forced marriage valid in God's eyes? Perhaps not. Aleksander did not think so. They had a great chat and got on very well.

Perhaps she'd fit in with the Brandts, after all. She stopped on the way home and bought a bunch of iris and gypsophilia for Claretta, who seemed very pleased, but was otherwise troubled.

"Sonja! . . . Posen!" was all Phoebe could understand of what she said to Aleksander.

"I knew she'd never stay! We will have to engage somebody else."

"I'll help to clean and cook," Phoebe said quickly. "That'll be my keep. But you'll have to teach me how to cook. I can't cook English, not to mind German! I have no idea how to cook *spätzle* or—or—*sauerkraut*! And I'll sleep in the attic room, if I can make it comfortable enough."

They all thought that it was worth a try.

Over the next six months, Phoebe learned everything very quickly. When she wasn't keeping house, she was training downstairs, tumbling on mats, hoisting herself up ropes, swinging from bar to bar. Her muscles had to be stronger, Claretta kept telling her. She tried tightrope walking, tried again and again and again after falling, determined to make progress. She accompanied Claretta to the music hall and saw her act and how it dazzled the audience. She was very proud to be introduced as the niece of *The Incomparable Claretta* to the cast and crew. She felt very much at home in the music hall and wished she'd grown up in the business.

"Phoebe is getting very good!" Claretta said, smiling. Her English was improving by the day. "I'm going to ask Mr. Fawcett if she can work with me!"

Phoebe glowed with happiness when Mr. Fawcett, an elderly rotund man in a green and white striped suit, agreed and suggested a sketch. He and Claretta wrote a comic piece in which she would train a new girl on the ropes, a novice who made funny errors. The risks to Phoebe were small, though she had to take some bumps, as she comically tried to emulate the more skilled artist. Phoebe found she had a gift for clowning, and engaged the audience very well, turning to them in mimed appeal in her various dilemmas, making them laugh.

The Brandts engaged a servant, and the landlord said he would have a vacant room above theirs in a week. She would take it. Everything was advancing in her favour, and she had not neglected her first family, even though her initial emotional reaction had been to forsake them completely.

Months ago, she'd written to Lowick, and her mother and Clara had written back. Her father, it seemed, was not speaking to her. She wrote him a letter of apology for running away but he still did not write or send a message. It hurt her.

Especially as she still thought of him as her father. Aleksander was more of a friend, in truth, or maybe an uncle. She felt happy for little Alex, though she thought his father drove him very hard, to tears sometimes. She'd protested on his behalf, but Aleksander had become offended with her, and told her it was the way to perfection. Phoebe tried to remember what it had been like for Claretta when she'd come out of the workhouse, the loss of her friends, trying to get used to a new life. But Alex seemed happy to be with his father, and when she asked him if he missed his friends in the workhouse, he said he could not remember them.

CHAPTER FIFTY

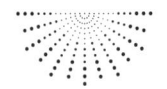

Phoebe's job went very well, and to her surprise, she forgot Tristam in a matter of weeks. A *lion comique* named Elliott Chandler, the Club's top billing act, was a handsome man with lazy hazel eyes. He began to take notice of Phoebe after about six weeks, and she was flattered. Before long, he was taking her out. She saw the envy of some of the other girls working there, particularly the singers. One singer in particular, Miss Woodfil, flirted with Mr. Chandler and was very snooty with Phoebe and any other members of the cast she considered inferior. Phoebe felt rather smug about snatching Mr. Chandler from under her nose. Aunt Claretta did not like him and warned her off.

"Why were you late home last night?" asked Aleksander one morning. "I heard your footsteps above, around three o'clock. I hope you were not with Mr. Chandler? Stay away from him; he has a bad name!" he thundered.

Phoebe did not listen to him. She was smitten. One night after the show, Elliott took her on a carriage drive around Victoria Park. They got out to see the moon, and he told her he loved her. He could wait for her no longer, and if she made him wait, he would go insane. She had to prove her love tonight. She went to his rooms, and from then on, they were lovers.

Aleksander was very angry at her even later hours, but she did not listen to him. He had no right to be angry. Did he not remember his own youth? At that, he stamped away.

One morning in May, Claretta had bad news for her. Mr. Fawcett had discontinued the double act. He had decided that Claretta was to do her act by herself, and that it would be as it was before.

"But why?" she demanded to know. "Everybody loved it! We're packing the house! I'll speak to Elliott," she added in an authoritative voice, certain of her influence over him. Elliot would make it right, she thought, for he could threaten to leave the club if she did not get her job back. He was the Star. They would never allow him to leave.

Aleksander banged his coffee cup down on the saucer and shook his head. Claretta looked on with pity as she took her coat and hat and left the flat.

She walked briskly to his lodgings at 45 Putnam Street—she knew her way there very well. As she turned the corner, she saw him go in and the big red front door shut behind him.

She pressed the doorbell, and his housekeeper, Mrs. Crimmins, answered.

"I'm sorry, he's not in," she said.

"Oh, but he is. I saw him come in a moment ago."

She looked confused.

"Just a moment," she said, and shut the door in her face.

She reappeared after a few minutes. Her face was flushed.

"I'm sorry. Mr. Chandler isn't in."

Phoebe was flabbergasted. She understood that he did not wish to see her, and she turned away dumbly. The door shut.

She went back home to her room and sat on the bed. She felt very ill. What had happened? Why did Elliott not want to see her? He loved her, didn't he? Surely, she was entitled to an explanation! That evening, she would go toward the Club and standing across the street, in the shadows, she would be able to intercept him on his way to work.

She stood there for some time, and finally saw him. He was arm-in-arm with Miss Woodfil, who was nestling against him. His head was bent to hers; they were sharing a private joke. She retreated into the shadows. Her tears blurred her way on her route home.

"He said he loved me," she said with great bitterness. "He didn't mean it! He used me!"

What would she do now? She had no income!

Aleksander became immediately worried, for Claretta declared her intention of leaving Fawcett Music Hall. She would not work for a man who treated one of the great Brandts so shabbily, all because his Star had tired of her! Claretta was also jealous that she was not billed higher than Chandler. Anybody with a voice could sing, she thought derisively, but what she did took years of training.

"You can come back to Prussia with us, if you wish," Aleksander said. "We will go as soon as we can, for my father is in frail health."

"You're going back so soon?" she gasped.

"I wish to see him. I wish him to know young Alexander."

"This was the father who made you marry Gertrud! I wonder you want to see him at all!" she exploded. "I would hate him, if I were you!"

"You cannot hate your father," he snapped. "Are you coming with us?"

"No, I don't want to go to Germany. And you didn't say you wanted your father to meet *me* anyway."

"You are right. I'm sorry. What will you do now?"

"I will go—*home*," she said it now, that Lowick was home. Papa would come around, she knew. She'd go home a different person and be a good, kind good-humoured daughter. She'd learned her lesson.

"I think you are wise," he said, kindly. "Your mother and your sister and brother are there."

Her eyes brimmed with tears.

"Now, don't weep. Some people have only one father, you have two! And both love you! Neither of us, I suspect, is perfect."

"Yes, he always has loved me!" she wept even harder. Aleksander patted her hand.

"Maybe you will come to Germany one day," he said. "I am so happy to have met you, and to know you, *tochter*. And allow me to give you a word of advise. Find a man who is worthy of you. I wish your mother's father had given her that advice."

"Don't say that. Good came out of it . . . me and little Alex!"

"Your poor Mama. If we could do things over—but there is no point in speaking like this. We cannot."

Phoebe made her way to Blackbell Cemetery and sat down by her mother's grave.

Dear Mama, I thought I knew everything and now I realise I know very little. I thought you were stupid. But I did the same thing you did. So, I understand at last. I understand so much more now than I did before. Rest in Peace, Mama.

Aleksander had had a modest stone made—*Dora Davis. Died 1875 aged 27. Deeply Mourned. Lord Have Mercy.* Phoebe placed a jar with silk violets against it and pushed the earth up around it, and a few small stones, to keep it in place.

CHAPTER FIFTY-ONE

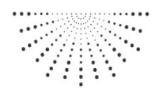

Clara could not leave her mother and father behind this year to pursue her intention of nurse training. Her father especially did not look well of late. He'd been listless since Phoebe left. He'd become bitter. He could hardly bear to hear her name mentioned. He did not read her letters. They were all about her *father*, that *Aleksander* fellow, who sired her and disappeared, only to reappear now when she was an adult. And she was *working*! Exhibiting herself on a public stage! What kind of father was Brandt, to allow her to do such a thing? Both parents were shocked and her mother in particular had very unflattering things to say of Aleksander.

Clara tried to explain to them that if it was respectable to perform in a circus it was surely respectable to perform in a music hall, and that even Royalty patronized the circus. No, they argued. The clientele for these music halls consisted of low, vulgar people. They were ashamed of Phoebe!

One day when the meadow was blossoming with poppies, Clara had happy news for them. She'd received a letter from London.

"Phoebe is coming home!" she said. Her mother's face lit up, her father looked up from his pudding and she saw a softening of his expression.

The Brandts are going back to Prussia and I have declined their invitation to accompany them there. I wish to come home to Lowick, if you will have me.

"Of course, we will!" said Mrs. Marshall.

"When is she to arrive?" asked Mr. Marshall eagerly.

"She doesn't say—she's helping them to pack and will see them off and close the flat in Hackney. Then she will come."

Her father looked very happy indeed.

"I knew she wouldn't like the Brandts!" he beamed. "She has nothing in common with them at all."

"We must tell the Epworths." Her mother said. "Lewis was ordained at Easter. His mother was very particular that Phoebe should know. They don't know her particular circumstances of course. . . ." She looked down and sighed.

CHAPTER FIFTY-TWO

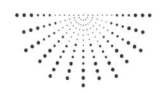

"When is she coming?" asked her father rather querulously. "It's been a month since we received her letter, and she's not here yet."

Clara shook her head. "I've written to the address in Hackney, and there hasn't been any reply. I'm sure she is all right Papa; don't worry."

But it was useless telling him, or her mother, not to worry. She was just as worried as they. She did not know what to do. Had something happened to Phoebe? If so, what? London was a dangerous place. There were murders there every week!

Perhaps Phoebe had a sweetheart, and he was the cause of her not returning. But she had not mentioned any admirer.

"I want to send Lionel there, to find her," Mr. Marshall said. "Something's happened to her. We have to find out. She's been robbed and has no money to come home. That's what it is. She has no money. Maybe she had to go back that that den of sin to earn some by exhibiting herself. Those Brandts may have had a very bad influence on her. Foreigners, too. They abandoned her. Did they not give her any money to get home? Mother! Mother!"

Mrs. Marshall came from her room where she had been praying.

"Will you send for Lionel, Mother? He must go to London tomorrow to look for Phoebe."

"Richard, Lionel cannot take time off school at this very moment. His headmaster is strict with the teachers."

"It's an Emergency!" said Mr. Marshall, getting up from the chair with an effort. "He shall go! Oh, what time is it? I have to do my round."

"I will do it for you tonight, dear, if Clara will do mine."

"I will, Mama."

Mr. Marshall sank heavily back on his chair.

"Phoebe has been robbed. We have to get the train fare to her, so that she can come home. My little Phoebe! Clara, go and write to Lionel, if your mother won't do it."

Clara took a deep breath. Phoebe, Phoebe, Phoebe! She loved her sister but since she had announced her intention of coming home, her father had been obsessing about the day and the hour. When the post brought no letter, he was constantly checking the window to see if she had caught the train from London and had gotten a lift from Sudford.

"Let me go to London," Clara heard herself say. She longed to go somewhere. But her mother and father were in such need of her! "Ask Aunt Jane to come!" she added, in an inspiration.

"You, you cannot go to London on your own!" her father would not hear of it.

"I don't have to go on my own," she said, her mind working rapidly. "Wait a few weeks, and Lionel will have holidays. It's better that two of us can go, and a woman can make enquiries of other women, and get better information. For women talk to women. Who knows, Phoebe might arrive in the meantime."

There was silence as they considered this.

"Very well," her father said. Still, the letter had to be written that very night, to Lionel, who lived in Sudford. A reply came by return post, he would of course go to London with Clara and they would find Phoebe.

CHAPTER FIFTY-THREE

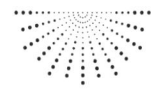

Aunt Jane came and settled in.

"I see a big change in your poor father," she said quietly to Clara. "He cannot go on working much longer. He will have to retire. If your father retires, your mother will have to retire as well. The Guardians are under no obligation to keep her on."

"Mamma would love to retire. I think Papa would find it a great ease also."

"They should purchase a cottage, or a small house. For if your father were to become incapacitated, the Guardians would suffer no delay in requiring him to vacate these rooms."

"Mamma reminds him of that at least once a week! But he wants to retire to the East End of London, or nowhere."

Jane shook her head. "They should have something in reserve, or they will end up renting an inferior house, wasting money they could have invested in a nice little property. I hope you and Lionel are able to see something of the city when you are there. Once you've found Phoebe and relieved her, of course. Now, will you take your white lawn? Will it travel well?"

"Yes, and the green plaid. It's sensible is it not? I hope to visit St. Thomas Hospital in Westminster and ask the Matron there if I can enter the Training School next year."

"Why, dear?"

"It used to be so I could help Mamma more, but now it's because I like working with people who are ill and in need of care."

"I think that is a very noble thing to do. I wish you all the best with it. Even if you marry and do not work, it is very useful knowledge."

CHAPTER FIFTY-FOUR

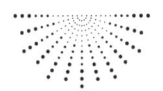

The train sped through the countryside and soon they reached London. They booked their own lodgings first, then went straight to the address in Hackney. The landlord was there.

"The Brandts went back to Germany. Who? The lady who lived with them, English? I remember her. Miss Davis, she was. Yes, Miss Davis. She rented a separate room. No, I don't know where she was working. There are three hundred music halls in this city. Sorry."

"She came 'ere from Whitechapel," chimed in a next-door neighbour, who was out sweeping the path in front of her house. "But I don't know if she went back there. I 'ope not. It's no place for a woman without protection, I say."

"We have nothing useful to go on," said Lionel, as they ate that evening at their boarding house. "What to do now?"

"We will have to search the music halls," Clara said. "I wish I had asked her the name of the one she was working in. The people there might know where she went, if she's left."

"I'll go to the music halls." Lionel said. "Mamma would have a fit if you went to one of those places."

"You won't get very far without me, Lionel."

"Of course, I will! I'm the brother."

"They won't believe you, as you're Mr. Marshall and she's going by Davis. But that's only one reason. I want to be able to question the women there; you can't do that. You don't know the right things to ask. Where shall we begin?"

Lionel got a map and laid it on the table. "Area by area," he said. "So let's try Hackney first, as we're here, and then Whitechapel perhaps."

That evening, they paid to get into the Cherry Music Hall and sat at one of the long tables. It was crowded and noisy. Neither had been in such a place before and looked around them awkwardly at first.

"Don't look so country-bumkinish," Clara whispered. "Act like we frequent these kinds of places all the time!"

The show began and in spite of a certain libertine air about the acts, they found themselves enjoying them very much, laughing at the swells, mesmerized by the electric tricks, awed when the trapeze artist flew above their very heads. They even sang along.

"I never enjoyed myself so much," Clara said. "But I keep looking for Phoebe, and she isn't here. Not in the acts, not serving drinks. It's time for me to ask someone if they know her."

Clara got up and approached a waitress. She shook her head. Phoebe Davis had never worked here.

On her way back to her own table, Clara heard a voice exclaim: "Claretta Davis! Is it you?" She swung around, to see a girl about her own age, tall and slim, with fair hair. Who could know her by the name Claretta Davis, after all these years? It had to be someone who knew her when she was a little girl! She saw the gentle expression and the smiling eyes.

"Alice Winter! Is it Alice?"

"Yes, yes! It's me! Oh, you are looking so well, Claretta!"

"I'm just Clara now. Clara Marshall. It's a long story!"

"Do you remember my brother, Thomas?" She indicated a gentlemanly young man beside her, with light brown hair, calm grey eyes and an open, pleasant countenance. He bowed his head.

"Why, yes! Your mother used to come and see you both. How is she?"

"She is very well. We left *that place*, you know, when I was ten. Mama's uncle left her a house in Shadwell, and we went to live there. Mama took in lodgers, and we've been there ever since. Thomas is in a business selling property; he's doing very well. We came here tonight because our cousin is in the show, he's the swell!"

"Oh, so talented! Come and meet my brother, Lionel. I have a long story to tell you . . ."

Lionel stood and shook hands with Clara's friends. As Clara related all that had happened to her and to the Marshall family in the last several years, Thomas and Alice were very interested. During the conversation, Alice and Lionel smiled at each other a great deal. Clara was so busy being intrigued by it, that she never noticed Thomas's gaze fixed upon her.

"We know London well; we'll help you find Phoebe. I well remember her performance on the wall that day in the workhouse! We talked about it for a long time, remember? What a story!"

CHAPTER FIFTY-FIVE

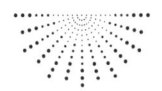

Lodgings were expensive. Alice suggested they move to their house, and their mother could rent them rooms at a cheaper rate. Lionel dashed off a letter to Lowick advising them of a change of address.

The return post brought disturbing news. The Board had decided that the Master of the Union Workhouse was no longer able to effectively carry out his duties. Mr. and Mrs. Marshall had to remove from the Master's Quarters. *Please look out for a small house for us in a quiet area,* Mrs. Marshall wrote. *We want to come back to Town. Nothing above 400 pounds. We are coming to London as soon as ever we can. Do not think of coming back to help us move. Please continue your search for Phoebe, both of you. Jane and two men that Rev. Epworth found for us are helping us pack.*

Thomas was the obvious person to appeal to here, and he began to search diligently for a suitable house in or near Blackbell.

The search for Phoebe went on, and the young people went out to the music halls, but nothing came of any enquiry.

Nobody knew Phoebe Davis, nor Phoebe Marshall. After visiting a dozen such establishments, they broadened their net to Lambeth, and entered the Fawcett Music Hall. Clara, while scanning the crowd, saw a handsome gent walking by. He looked at her and winked, and her heart turned over. He was aged about thirty, had hazel eyes and an impertinent smile. He disappeared, only to appear onstage later in costume, and give several spirited renderings of old and new favourites, finishing with the tender *Love's Old Sweet Song*. Lights lowered, he descended and walked among the audience. Clara's heart skipped a beat when he approached; she looked down, but when she looked up again, he was before her, singing to her. He winked again and moved along, leaving her in a kind of dizzy confusion. She heard no more for the rest of the evening. Lionel and Alice were deep in conversation; Thomas could not come this night.

But she could not be deflected from her enquiries about Phoebe, so she left her place after the show was over and approached a songstress who was now drinking a glass of wine with her friends.

"Excuse me," she said politely. "I wonder if you could help me. I'm searching for a friend who may have worked here, Phoebe Davis, or perhaps she's known as Marshall."

At last! A reaction that was not a regretful shake of the head.

"She used to work here," said the songstress. "Look, Mr. Chandler had a—passing acquaintance with her, did you not, Elliott?" she threw her eyes toward the man approaching the table. Clara's knees felt weak. It was him again! He gave her an admiring glance before he turned his attention to the questioner.

"What did you say, Bella? Who did I have a passing acquaintance with?"

"Miss Phoebe Davis. Did you know her, or not? This lady is looking for her." Clara detected a slight tone of mockery. Mr. Chandler was standing next to her—too close. She felt his presence acutely. Part of her wished to move away, but she seemed under a spell.

"Miss Davis. She used to work here with her aunt. She went back to Germany with her." He offered.

"No, that's incorrect," Clara heard herself say.

He pulled out a chair with a flourish.

"Please, Miss, be seated." He bowed to her.

Clara had never encountered such attention. She hesitated only a moment—she did not know any of the company, but Lionel and Alice were engrossed in each other and these people knew Phoebe! It was not a time for formalities.

"Miss—?" he seated himself beside her and turned his enthralling eyes upon her.

"Miss Marshall."

"And Miss Davis was your friend? I'm sorry we don't know anything more than what I have told you, but if you could perhaps expand a little, maybe something will come to mind."

"She wrote to us that she was working at night as an acrobat."

"We'd like to know what became of her too," said a woman with very red lip colour. "She left very suddenly, as did my emerald ring the last night she was here."

"Cornelia," said Mr. Chandler in reproof. "You're always losing things. I'm sorry." He said to Clara.

"Phoebe is no thief!" Clara said, reddening.

"Thief?" Lionel was at the table, and Alice behind him.

"Phoebe worked here!" Clara explained. "When did she leave?" she asked Mr. Chandler.

"Several weeks ago. They discontinued the act she was in." Bella said.

"She went to Germany, with the Brandts. Her relations." Mr. Chandler insisted.

"No, she decided not to go with them. She was coming home to us, to Sudford." Lionel said, wanting to take over the enquiry. "But what we need to know is, where is my sister now?"

They looked from face to face in front of them, but with sinking hearts. Nobody seemed to be able to help with that information. Instead, Mr. Chandler asked them to sup with him. Clara was disappointed that Lionel declined. But he had to take Alice home early or her mother would be angry.

"We shall meet again," Mr. Chandler said to Clara as he took her hard in farewell. "As to how, and where, is up to you. You're the lady."

"I thought the gentleman was supposed to arrange meetings." Clara said, hardly believing her own boldness. And her own luck.

"May I ask where you are lodging, then?"

She gave him the address in Shadwell.

"With your permission, I will call upon you tomorrow," he said. "At three o'clock. In the meantime, perhaps something else may occur to me as to the possibility of Miss Davis's whereabouts."

Clara went home in a dream. Mr. Chandler's spellbinding eyes were before her. His voice echoed in her ears. And she thought that perhaps he knew more about Phoebe than he was telling her. Perhaps Phoebe had confided in him?

CHAPTER FIFTY-SIX

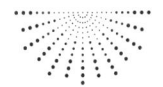

The following morning saw Clara in a heightened state. She spent an hour doing her hair, thought it looked truly dreadful, and redid it. She took out all her clothes and decided none of them would do. They were all ugly, old-fashioned, and provincial. Finally, she decided on her white cotton lawn with pink rosebuds for her all-important visitor, who came promptly at three.

"You look ravishing," was his greeting, which caused her heart to flutter. They were in the parlour. She felt suddenly, inexplicably guilty. Why was she falling in love when Phoebe was missing?

"About Phoebe," she said. "Have you remembered anything else?"

"I do not. But—I have some information."

"What is it?" she eagerly asked, sitting down suddenly, indicating he should do the same.

"She was seeing a gentleman—a man who has since left London."

Clara looked bewildered.

"He used her abominably."

Clara began to feel the weight of such a statement.

"Was she in love with him?"

"I am afraid so. Her father disapproved."

"Was this man a friend of yours, that you knew this?"

"We shared a dressing room. He was a talkative kind of fellow."

"What was his name?"

"I'm not at liberty to disclose that. I'm sorry."

"It seems that it would be no harm to disclose it to me," she said, after a pause. "Are you saying that she did not go back to Germany after all?" she frowned.

"I have been thinking the matter further. She was distraught at the separation. Would you like to come for a carriage ride with me? We can talk with more freedom outside. Regents Park is splendid at this time of year."

The door opened just then, and Thomas Winter stood there. He seemed surprised, mumbled an apology, and shut the door immediately.

"Who's that?"

"Mr. Winter, the man of the house."

"He doesn't like me." He gave her a telling look. "Shall we go?"

"I shall just tell my brother I'm going out."

"Tell your brother! Some women your age are married!"

Clara slipped out of the room. She stopped in the hall and took a deep breath. There was something odd about Mr. Chandler and his story. And somehow, he did not seem half as handsome as he had last night. He seemed slippery. She went to the back parlour and told the others where she was going.

"I think he knows more than what he is disclosing," she said.

"I'm not entirely at ease with you going with him," frowned Lionel.

"Nor me. These theatre types can be tricky gamesters," glowered Thomas.

"Clara, are you sure?" Alice said, "I can come too, you know."

"No, you stay with your original plan." They had decided today to walk around the centre of Town, searching.

She took her straw bonnet with the pink ribbon from the rack. She glanced in the mirror. What a waste of time this morning had been!

Mr. Chandler drove his own phaeton, a smart new model. Clara resolved to keep her eyes open everywhere for Phoebe.

"How long do you plan to stay in London?" he asked.

"Until we find Phoebe."

"And if you do not?"

"I'm sure we will. She's here somewhere. She must be."

"You don't think she could be—dead or anything, do you?"

"Of course, that's something we thought of, accidents can happen—but the chances are slight, and the police would have contacted us."

"If they have no identification on them, nobody ever knows. And the Thames is full of bodies. Despairing young women, mostly."

Clara thought the conversation had taken a chilling turn.

"We are not thinking about that. As far as we're concerned, she's alive. And Phoebe isn't the type to despair."

"Have you been to the police?"

"Lionel went there, but they say there are so many women reported missing in London, that they can't do anything. Still, they took a description."

"Here's the park. Shall we walk in, or would you like to drive about it?"

"Can we walk? It's a beautiful day for a walk."

He handed his phaeton to the care of a boy and they went into the park. They walked about the beautiful grounds for an hour or so, admired the gardens, and as they walked down a tree-lined pathway, Clara noted they were quite alone.

Suddenly Mr. Chandler pulled her toward the trees and tried to kiss her. She tried to protest, and wrestle herself away, but he was too strong. Her hat came off, her hair was down.

"Get away from her!" Thomas was suddenly there, pulling him off her.

"The landlord's boy!" said Chandler. "No need to get all angry like that, son. The lady likes me."

"I objected strongly!" said Clara hotly.

"I learned to fight when I was knee high to a grasshopper, and you'll feel my fists if you don't 'op along," said Thomas.

Chandler left, with a sneer.

"Are you all right?" asked Thomas.

She smoothed her gown. "Yes, I'm fine. Nasty fellow! A cad! He knows something about Phoebe. He wants us to believe her dead. He wants us to stop looking—why would he want us to stop looking, Thomas?"

Thomas did not reply. The sunlight poured on his hair and he seemed like a knight in shining armour to her at that moment. How had she thought the cad handsome?

"I don't know," Thomas said. They walked back along the path, Clara trying to tuck her hair, under her hat.

"When I saw you with him in our front parlour, I thought you liked him, but then you seemed to be aware he was a bad one when you came to talk to us," Thomas said then.

"Did you know he was a bad one, then?"

"He has a reputation, yes. There are rumours about him."

"What kinds of rumours?"

"Very bad rumours. That he killed his wife. Here are the others." Lionel and Alice were standing closely together at the entrance to the path.

"You all followed me?"

"My idea, Clara," Alice said apologetically. "And I sent Tom after you down this path."

"So the cad may have killed his wife, did he? Now I'm frantic about Phoebe!" Clara said.

CHAPTER FIFTY-SEVEN

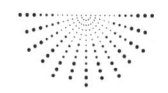

Weeks went by. Summer in London was getting uncomfortable. Clara helped Mrs. Winter with housekeeping, and Lionel with gardening. Lionel was officially courting Alice. As there would be no more family in Lowick, he tendered his resignation to the school at Sudford, and looked for a post in or near London.

Thomas found a house, two bedrooms upstairs, two rooms downstairs, and a small kitchen. It faced Blackbell Green which gave it a pretty aspect. The price was satisfactory, and the family prepared to remove there as soon as possible. Lionel found a position as schoolteacher near Bromley.

They still searched for Phoebe. But there were no leads. She seemed to have vanished from the face of the earth. The police had little hope of locating her.

One question occupied Clara's mind. What if poor Phoebe was with child? Where would she go?

The workhouse of course, as her mother had had to do.

It broke her heart to have to go about to the workhouses looking for Phoebe. Whitechapel, Hackney, Spitalfields, Lambeth, Bethnal Greene, and so on . . . Blackbell was the last one she and Lionel tried. They thought it unlikeliest of all that they should find her in the place she was born and had been known for her years there as Miss Phoebe. They trudged there one hot afternoon. They met several people who remembered them, and Mr. Bateman told them that the last time he saw Phoebe she had been looking for her mother's address. No, she was not an inmate. Of that he was sure.

CHAPTER FIFTY-EIGHT

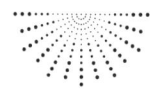

The Marshalls settled in. They were glad to be retired; her mother especially. Her father was very pleased to be back in London. If only they could find Phoebe!

An early visitor in their new abode was Rev. Lewis Epworth. He was a new curate at a parish near Bromley and was pleased to hear that Lionel would not be far away. He had visited, hoping to see Phoebe, and was very disturbed to hear that she was missing. He too became determined to find out what had become of her.

If Thomas had business in the area, he always dropped in. "I'm still suspicious of Chandler," Clara said to him one day when she poured him tea. Her father and mother had gone for a quiet stroll on the green. "I want to go to the police, but I don't think they'll listen to me. Where does he live? Have his rooms ever been searched? Perhaps he's holding Phoebe prisoner there. Now we have these murders in Whitechapel, and I'm more nervous than ever."

An idea she could give no expression to had come into her head. If Phoebe was destitute, had she turned to the unthinkable? She'd heard that many women who came to London with high hopes found themselves on the streets. She could give no voice to her concern. And she could not go to those areas herself to search, and certainly not at night. Women of the night were being targeted by someone the newspapers were calling Jack the Ripper. Could Phoebe have become an as-yet-undiscovered victim? She dared not mention her thoughts to anybody.

"Will you come for a walk on Sunday?" Thomas asked her. "I want to scout out a house in Blackbell to show on Monday."

She agreed. She hoped that Thomas liked her more than any other girl he knew. He seemed to do a lot of business in Blackbell, and that might be a good sign.

The house was by the cemetery, and on their way home they decided to take a shortcut through it. Though it was far from a romantic setting, Thomas took her hand as they walked up a grassy path.

"Look!" Clara exclaimed. "Dora's grave! The woman who robbed me of my birthright for eight years," she added in a quieter tone, with just a hint of sadness.

She saw something glitter among the wilted bouquets there. She rummaged and picked up an ivory diamante comb, discoloured badly by crusted brown stains.

"That's Phoebe's! Why is this here? Something happened, Tom. We have to go to the police. Oh, please don't let those stains be—you know!"

"Wait a moment, no need to think the worst," Thomas urged her quietly. "Perhaps she laid her head down there in grief, and the comb came out of her hair. The stains are just from the vegetation."

Clara shook her head. "I don't know! Perhaps she was hurt here, on this very spot!"

CHAPTER FIFTY-NINE

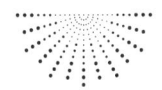

The constable went into a back room and returned with a ledger. He turned the pages ever so slowly and Clara's fingers itched to pull it from him and read it herself.

"Let me see—entries for Blackbell Cemetery this summer —*young man found intoxicated having imbibed, said he thought he was on a ship and the tombstones were other ships—*"

Clara's fingers itched even more.

"*. . . 'fight broken up outside Blackbell Cemetery, Mr. Alfred Shores and Mr. Charles Shores had that day buried their grandmother and there was a row over the funeral costs with Mr. Alfred stating that as their grandmother had left Mr. Charles all her money he, Mr. Alfred should not have to pay a farthing.'* Sounds fair enough, doesn't it?" he raised his eyes briefly to them.

Clara took a deep breath. Thomas squeezed her hand and winked.

"A lot of things happen in Blackbell Cemetery—ah! '*June 2$^{nd.}$ Woman found in a confused state, wandering outside gate, with a* *gash to back of head. No bag or reticule. Robbery. Unable to state name, address, or anything about herself except the name—'* he squinted. "It's very hard to read it, I can hardly make it out, it was Constable McFadden who wrote it, he should have been a doctor, his writing's that bad."

"Please can we look?" Clara implored, leaning forward.

"Oh, now this is confidential, Miss. All confidential. It looks like—*Faucalt* or *Fawcett*."

"The music hall!" exclaimed Thomas.

"What happened to her?" asked Clara fearfully.

"She was taken by police to St. Thomas Hospital, and we don't know anything else." He shut the ledger, leaving Clara cross.

"Did it say what age she was? What she was wearing? Look, I found my sister's comb. Is this blood?"

"Perhaps so, Miss."

CHAPTER SIXTY

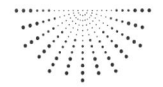

"St Thomas Hospital." Thomas said to the cab driver. They set off at a good pace. It was not very far away.

"So, this is St. Thomas!" said Clara, who even in her worry about Phoebe, could find a moment to admire the great building. "This is where I have thought of training as a nurse!"

"You're going to work?" Thomas asked, a little crestfallen.

"I will have to do something! Mamma and Papa can't keep me my whole life!"

He squeezed her hand. She liked it, his grip was firm and yet gentle. He managed to say a lot in those squeezes, she thought.

In the hospital, an orderly directed them to a chair in Dr. Snodgrass's office.

"We're searching for a woman admitted here on 2nd of June," said Clara. "She had a head wound and didn't know who she was. The woman we're looking for is young, my age, has red-gold hair and brown eyes, she's small in stature, slim."

"Are you a relative—?"

"Her sister. My name is Miss Clara Marshall."

"And this gentleman is—?"

"A friend of the family." Clara smiled at Tom.

Another squeeze of her hand, out of the doctor's view. He approved the description, or maybe he wanted to be more than a friend of the family . . . she squeezed back.

He called a secretary, Miss Todd, from a back office. Again, a ledger was produced. Miss Todd began to thumb slowly through it.

"*2nd June – 1:18am Young woman, unable to state her name, diagnosis: Intoxication.*" She said with triumph, shoving it in front of Dr. Snodgrass's nose."

"No," said he, "This woman had a head injury."

"It doesn't say she didn't have a head wound, Dr. Snodgrass," said the querulous Miss Todd.

Dr. Snodgrass took the book away and the secretary stalked back to her own office. He thumbed through the register. "This might be the woman you're looking for. '*2nd June 8:15pm Brought in by police, sent to Surgical Ward for Suturing of Scalp and Observation. Young woman. Unable to give name.*'"

"Anything else?"

"We wouldn't take a description or anything like that. We have to get her medical records now. There will be a great deal more I can tell you from that." To Clara's desperation, he called the secretary again, who being offended, took her time about appearing.

"Medical Records for *Unknown Female* please."

The door opened, a nurse popped her head in and told Dr. Snodgrass he was needed at the Pavilion this instant, if he pleased. He excused himself with a bow and handed the chart to the secretary.

Miss Todd looked smug.

"Oh, she was discharged to a Home for the Mentally Disturbed, called Lily Hill House. The address is Lily Hill, Wimbledon."

Mentally Disturbed?

"Is there anything else?" Clara asked. "Mr. Snodgrass said he could tell a great deal more from the chart—"

"Oh, come back another day if you want to know more about her. I'm very busy." Miss Todd left the room, taking the folder with her.

"It's too late to set off for Wimbledon now," said Clara, crestfallen.

"I can come with you tomorrow afternoon, after I've shown the house." Tom said.

CHAPTER SIXTY-ONE

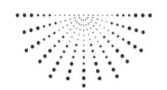

Lily Hill House was a neat Georgian building with balconies at every window visible from the road. The gate was locked, but a gatekeeper opened it upon hearing they were visitors. On this fine day, the patients were sitting out on the front lawn in the shade of several elm trees. A few nurses moved among them, administering medicine or adjusting rugs for the older people in bath-chairs.

As they walked up the avenue, Clara saw a slim young woman with red-gold hair sitting at a table with a few others. She hurried across the lawn in her direction.

"Phoebe!" she cried, her eyes wide with joy at first, followed by alarm, for there was no answering recognition in Phoebe's eyes, only bewilderment.

"Do you know Mrs. Fawcett?" said a nurse who had immediately appeared.

"Mrs. Fawcett?" Clara was aghast.

"Well yes, this is Mrs. Fawcett."

"She is not married!" Clara said.

"And who are you, Miss?"

"I'm her sister, Clara Marshall."

"Mrs. Fawcett, do you know Clara Marshall?" asked the nurse.

Phoebe shook her head slowly.

"No, Nurse Grayling."

"I'm sorry, but her husband has to approve her visitors," Nurse Grayling said, advancing on them to usher them away.

Clara was close to tears. She was so, so relieved that Phoebe was alive, but she'd never imagined she'd be like this!

"What about Mama, Papa, and Lionel? And—Aleksander—?" asked Clara with eagerness.

Phoebe shook her head mournfully.

"And Claretta?"

"Claretta! *The Incomparable Claretta!*" Phoebe raised her head in delight.

"Yes, and *The Amazing Aleksander.*"

"The Circus!" said Phoebe suddenly, but then she burst into tears.

"Look what you have done," said Nurse. "I must ask you again to take your leave. Now you have upset her."

Clara felt she had lost her voice; she made an effort to speak, but Thomas, seeing her confusion, interrupted.

"Now just a minute, Nurse," he said. "You heard Miss Marshall say this lady wasn't married. And she heard from her just before she disappeared, didn't you, Clara?"

"Yes, I did." Clara recovered herself. "She announced her intention of coming home to Mamma and Papa. She never arrived, and we set out to look for her."

An elderly doctor approached with hasty steps.

"What's this fuss? Did I hear you say she isn't married? She is married," he said flatly. "She's been married two years."

"That's wrong!" Clara began to shout. Thomas put his arm about Clara and glared at the doctor.

"We must ask you to leave now, and not return," the doctor said.

"We will return, and with the police," threatened Thomas. "Phoebe was living with her father until recently. She is not married." There was no need to tell them that there were two fathers in Phoebe's life.

They saw some brawny men running from the house toward them. Not wanting Clara to be manhandled by these brutish thugs, Thomas led her toward the gate.

"Ask this fellow Fawcett to produce a marriage certificate!" he shouted over his shoulder.

"Fawcett again. He owns the music hall, doesn't he?" Clara said on the platform waiting for the train. "She couldn't have married him since she went missing, could she? Could she have done it in secret?"

"We have to pay another visit to the music hall tonight," he said. "Are you going to tell your parents you found her?"

"Not until I have ascertained the truth of this. They would be even more upset than I, and I'm upset enough!"

They returned home to Blackbell; Clara announced that she was going to Alice Winters's house for the night, which was not at all a lie, since Thomas had proposed that she stay with them, so that they could stay late at the music hall. Before she went out, she wrote a letter to Lionel at Bromley to tell him the latest news. He had moved there already at the Headmaster's request, to oversee the repair of the old school during the holidays. Thomas engaged a reliable cab driver to deliver it to him first thing Tuesday morning.

CHAPTER SIXTY-TWO

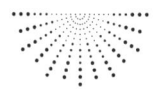

There he was, *lion comique* Elliott Chandler, performing on the stage. Slick and suave! That's what she thought of him now! She looked at Thomas. He was far more handsome than Elliott.

But where could they find Mr. Fawcett? And how could they broach the subject of whether he had married Phoebe?

After the song, Elliott made a bee-line for their table. *He cannot wait to find out why we are here,* thought Clara. *One would think he'd wish to avoid us!*

"And how's the landlord's boy?" he began. "Is there any particular reason why you're honouring me with a visit?"

"Well chap, it's not to see you to begin with," said Thomas, his eyebrow raised. "In fact, it's none of your business, is it? It's a free country, we can go where we like." He drummed his fingers on the table and looked beyond Chandler.

"Enchanted, I'm sure," Chandler nodded to Clara and disappeared.

Clara spotted a bald old rotund man in a striped suit walking about greeting people.

"That's Fawcett! I bet! Ooh, she could not have married him! He's sixty if he's a day!"

"Will you be all right here if I go and talk to him? Man to man."

"Of course."

Clara watched him approach the old gentleman, who bid him to follow him. She looked about her, not wanting to catch anybody's eye, but could not help seeing two women looking at her. She was not surprised therefore when they approached her. After the necessary introductions, one of them said that she'd seen her making enquiries about Miss Davis and thought there was something she ought to be aware of.

"Perhaps you know that Miss Davis and Mr. Chandler were lovers," one said. "He ended it as he ends it with all of the new girls, suddenly and without explanation. We felt sorry for her, she's young, and we know what he's like.

"As for her disappearance—I met her one day in a shop in Pryor Street, and we had a bit of a chat. She said she had lost an earring in Chandler's flat and she was going to go back to look for it, and she asked me what his night off was so she wouldn't go that night. I advised her not to go back to his flat. What's an earring? He's very devious, that man, and there are rumours—" she hesitated.

"Can you tell me what they are?" asked Clara, perturbed. She knew she should not ask people for rumours that took a person's character away, but in this circumstance, she had no scruple, and she wondered if it was the same rumour that Thomas had told her about.

"His wife was riding a bicycle down a hill and was frightened by a dog who ran in front of her. She went over the handlebars and was killed instantly. These penny-farthings are dangerous but there were suspicions."

"Why were there suspicions?"

"She'd confided in friends that if something happened to her, they should look for the cause in her husband. And it was well known she was terrified of dogs."

"How horrible! But do you think Miss Davis might have found out something about that?"

"If she was in his rooms looking for her earring, she may have come by something innocently. That's why we decided to speak with you, Miss Marshall."

Clara kept it to herself that they had found Phoebe. They had no more to say, and Tom was coming back.

CHAPTER SIXTY-THREE

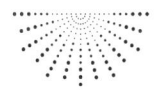

"Come away now," he said. He looked tense as he ushered her out the door.

"Mr. Fawcett—that old fellow—is a widower. But here's something interesting – Chandler is his nephew. His real name is Fawcett. Chandler is his stage name."

"A Fawcett! But—did they marry?"

"Fawcett is not aware that they did. I have to say I found the fellow very cagey. I don't like his eyes. I say, fancy a late supper?"

"Oh yes." They went to a little café where they took a corner table and ordered tea and sausage rolls.

Clara told him what she had learned. Thomas listened intently, then said:

"Perhaps he declared her insane to destroy her credibility. Our finding her is going to lead to all sorts of complications for him. Especially if there was no marriage because he has no authority over her anymore."

"Is there any way of finding out? Where would the marriage have been registered?"

"I wouldn't know where to begin in a city this size. Perhaps there's another way. It's time to go to the police again and to ask them to check this. They can do it quicker."

"Not if it's the constable we met before."

"We'll go back tomorrow and ask for the policeman who investigated his wife's accident. If he had any doubts about it, he'll be interested in this."

On their way to the police station on Tuesday, Clara voiced what had kept her awake the night before.

"I'm so afraid, Tom, that our finding her yesterday, and asking questions, could put her in more danger than before."

"I thought of that too," he said. "But we'll get everybody we know to help us check parish registers." He squeezed her hand, in reassurance this time.

Inspector Terry was very interested. He remembered the bicycle accident well and had had his suspicions. He thought this present development was worth looking into. Miss Davis suffered a gash to the head? How did she get that? Lily Hill was an expensive place to be. This Fawcett man must be wealthy, if he was shelling out for it. But they could be very successful, these music hall stars.

"Nothing else about Phoebe?" Mr. Marshall had asked that morning, as he did every day. "If only I was young enough, I'd scour London for my daughter."

"Nothing to tell you, Papa, I'm afraid." Clara felt dreadful withholding information. But he'd go to Wimbledon without delay if he knew, and Phoebe might be in even more danger.

Thomas dropped in that evening. He and Clara took a walk across the green.

"The Inspector got some men on the job. So far, no marriage registered. He made it up, or else went outside the Greater London Area."

"Thank Heaven for that! Now what do we do?"

CHAPTER SIXTY-FOUR

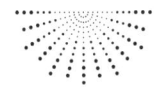

Phoebe woke up and saw the nurse, as always, at her bedside. There was nothing she could do while she was there.

She wondered how long she could keep up this pretense for. It had been so dreadfully difficult when she'd seen Clara running across the lawn toward her. The look on Clara's face when she did not get an answering cry of welcome, and no recognition, almost broke her heart. Nurse Grayling had been upon them immediately.

As long as Elliott thought she had lost her memory, she felt safe, until he got tired of paying for her asylum. He was probably wondering what to do with her. To have one wife die under suspicious circumstances was bad, to have two could put a noose around his neck.

It had begun when she found out she had left an earring at Elliott's flat. She admitted to herself that she didn't really care about the earring, she just wanted to go back to his flat and be miserable there for a while, hug his pillow and tell it how much she loved him and how he had deeply hurt her.

Broken hearts do funny things. One night she persuaded Mrs. Crimmins to allow her in for a few minutes. She searched on the carpet and under the bed and put her hand on a stack of papers. She'd withdrawn them and under the light of the lamp, examined them. They were newspaper cuttings from 1884 about a tragic accident. The wife of Mr. Elliott Fawcett, otherwise known as Elliott Chandler, the popular *lion comique*, was killed on Baker Hill when she was thrown from her bicycle after being frightened by a dog. She'd never even known he was married, let alone that his wife had died in this terrible accident. And his real name was Fawcett! Had he thought so little of her, that he didn't think her worthy of the knowledge?

She felt duped by him. She'd given him everything, expecting him to marry her, for when a man loves a woman, as he declared he did, and takes her virtue, was he not intending the security of marriage? She felt betrayed.

She rummaged through more papers, some more cuttings, and then found, folded up into several pieces, a handwritten note.

Baker Hill. Someone to hold dog until moment is right. Someone across street to whistle. Dog owner best for this. Grant Alley crosses Baker Hill halfway down.

There was a handwritten drawing, a rough sketch to illustrate the geography of Baker Hill with Grant Alley criss-crossing it.

Phoebe felt ill when she realised what this was. What would she do now? Go to the police?

A juicy bone for Horatio! was scribbled at the end.

She'd been so engrossed she hadn't heard the housekeeper come up to see what was taking her so long finding an earring. Mrs. Crimmins had opened the door and saw her sitting on the mat, stricken with her own distress. She coughed. Phoebe had shoved the papers back in under the bed and hurried to her feet.

Crimmins must have informed Elliott.

She knew it was Mr. Fawcett from the Club who had coshed her at Dora's grave, because she recognised the perfumed macassar oil he used on the few hairs he had left upon his head. But the sound of nearby voices frightened him off, and she managed to get herself up and staggered down the path and out the gate, her head bleeding. She'd felt very dizzy and confused, and afraid she would faint and not wake up, someone had called a bobby, and she'd said his name to him. *Their* name. Fawcett.

The next few days were very hazy. Then Elliott had appeared at her bedside, referring to her as *my wife*. He appeared to be a devoted husband. She was very frightened of him now. She thought her best defence would be to pretend amnesia. If he thought she had forgotten what she'd read, she might be safe, until she could think of a plan. Then she was moved here, to this place.

Every day she'd pretend to look out aimlessly the window, but she was really casing the drainpipes, railings, and balconies which would get her to the ground and out of the building. There was a locked gate; that would be no trouble to scale. But where would she go then?

And was her life in more danger now that Clara had visited? She shouldn't have "remembered" Aunt Claretta and Aleksander and the circus, but the heartbreak in Clara's voice was such that she could not refuse her a little joy. Then she'd burst into tears with the emotion of it all, and they'd blamed Clara for that . . . it had been a bit unwise to "remember" anything at all. If they thought her memory was coming back . . .

How odd it was that a few weeks ago she would have given anything to be Elliott's wife and now that her eyes had been opened to his character, she wanted to be as far away from him as she could be.

CHAPTER SIXTY-FIVE

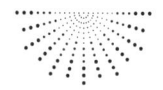

Rev. Lewis Epworth alighted the train and walked quickly toward Lionel Marshall's lodgings. He'd been making his own enquiries, calling at hospitals and convent hospices for young women, but nobody had ever known a Phoebe Marshall. He had called to Blackbell Green this morning in hopes of further news.

He'd loved Phoebe for years, and today he'd been told that she was not in fact a Marshall, and the entire tragic tale surrounding her birth was known to him. It did not make any difference to him that Phoebe was not born in wedlock. It might to a lot of people, even to his parishioners. She was the same as any other child of God. There was no need for this information to reach anyone else in his life, not even his parents.

After visiting the Marshalls, he decided to seek out Lionel, as they lived not far from one another in Bromley.

Lionel was very happy to see his old friend from Lowick. He showed him a long letter from Clara noting all the events since Sunday. They set off immediately to Wimbledon. Lewis was confident that his collar would gain him admittance to Lily Hill House, and so it was. A few hours later, he could hardly believe that he was seeing Miss Marshall—or the supposed Mrs. Fawcett—before his eyes, sitting out in the sunshine with the other patients.

Unlike Clara, he would not pretend any recognition, but move from patient to patient to minister to them. He reflected that there was a great need for his services here. He saw many sad, lonely, disturbed souls, their illnesses manifest in their eyes, in their drooping physiques, their apathy at even this beautiful day God had surrounded them with. Perhaps their families had abandoned some of them.

If he could come here often, Phoebe or not, it would be a blessing for him to be able to help these poor people.

He took his time, for the patients were in need of a person to say a kindly word, or to pray with them. They brightened up at the sight of this young man with the big smile. He was caring and joyful. More than one patient began to feel rays of healing sunshine into their hearts.

The staff took no notice of the clergyman. Lewis was very careful not to glance in Phoebe's direction after he had first seen her. He did not know whether she had seen him or not; it didn't matter. She had lost her memory. If she hadn't known Clara, she would not know him. In the meantime, he was well occupied. An elderly gentleman was telling him the sad story of how he had come to be there. He stilled the anxiety that Phoebe would get up and go inside and that he might miss her. At this moment, he was where God wished him to be, by this troubled gentleman's side. He would trust in whatever God had planned for him today.

CHAPTER SIXTY-SIX

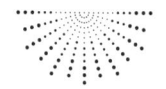

I t couldn't be, thought Phoebe, watching the black-garbed young man with the white collar moving about from patient to patient. It couldn't be—but it was! It was Lewis Epworth!

He doesn't know I'm here. If he comes up and greets me, what shall I do? Pretend not to know him?

He is coming this way! He cannot but see me now!

He passed by.

Was it not Lewis after all? Of course, it was—she'd known him since they were children. But why did he not greet her—suddenly the truth hit.

He knows! His visit here today is no accident! He thinks I've lost my memory and don't recognise him.

She almost laughed aloud at the funny implications of this. If her situation was not so serious, she could play a good joke on him. Instead, she had to find out how to use this situation to her advantage.

"Nurse!" she called out. Nurse Grayling was at her side in a moment.

"May I have a word with the clergyman?" she asked in a hushed voice. "I would so like to unburden myself and receive a blessing."

Nurse Grayling assented. There was no rule that patients could not speak to a spiritual counsellor. She indicated an empty bench a few yards away where she might be seated, and when she was there, sent Lewis over. He sat down by her side, without any hint that he knew her.

When the nurse was out of hearing, she whispered: "Lewis. I haven't lost my memory. My life is in danger."

His heart leaped when he heard her say his name. Her next words had astonished him, washing his heart in waves of delight. But the last sentence had plunged his heart into turmoil.

"You've been talking to Clara, yes?" she whispered.

"I'm up to date," Lewis inclined his bowed head toward her and nodded sagely as if acknowledging her sins. "How can we help you?"

"I can escape from this place tonight, if you or somebody could be outside the gate, to meet me before I'm missed. About eleven o'clock."

"Is that the only way?"

"What's wrong with it?"

"I was thinking of sending the police to fetch you out, since you aren't married, your next-of-kin is your father."

"Oh, how did you know I wasn't married? I think they nearly convinced Clara I was."

"The police checked; we checked. Everybody's been working hard since yesterday. I live at Bromley Rectory now. Do more talking. You're supposed to be telling me your sins."

"If you knew them, you'd walk away from me."

Lewis felt instantly sorry.

"Nothing could make me walk away from you. You mustn't think about them any longer. If you ask God's forgiveness, your sins dissolve like ink under running water. God loves to forgive." He longed to take her hand in his.

"I'm a ruined woman."

"No, stop. I love—" he stopped. What had come over him? Now was not the time to declare himself!

"Tonight, you say?"

"Nurse Grayling goes off duty at eight, and I'm not watched at night. Unless Elliott comes tonight, I will be alone and able to get away. Oh, here's Doctor Fry. He's very suspicious of everybody. Or protective maybe, I can't make up my mind. Bless me now."

He did so and rose. He saw the doctor look at him with wariness.

CHAPTER SIXTY-SEVEN

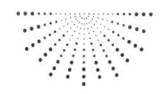

"You saw a clergyman today, didn't you?" said Elliott, later, after sending Nurse Grayling away.

"Yes. He heard my confession."

"What's his name?"

"He never said his name."

"I'm getting worried, Phoebe. They know where you are. Maybe even *you* know who you are, and where you are, and why you're here?"

Phoebe was silent.

Chandler paced the room. "This place is rotten expensive. Tomorrow you're going to Bedlam. Nobody will believe anything you have to say, though, in there, about me. By the way, someone has been asking Uncle questions. He's very nervous."

"Was Horatio his dog?" asked Phoebe. She saw no reason to keep up the pretense now.

"Ah! You were deceiving us, all. You are a good actress. A talent wasted. Yes, Horatio was my uncle's dog. My cousin Bert held him, and then across the street Uncle whistled for him to come as soon as he saw Mary freewheeling down the hill. I planned the perfect murder."

"How can it be a perfect murder, when God knows about it?"

The door was thrown open and two of Her Majesty's Police burst in.

"I believe we've met before, Mr. Fawcett?" said the older of the two.

"Inspector Terry!"

"I'm placing you under arrest for the murder of your wife on October 12th 1884."

"This is ridiculous! The inquest said it was an accident! I was nowhere about!"

"We paid your uncle a visit today. He confessed to being a part of it, in return for his life." They tied his hands behind his back. "And we were just outside the door when we heard your boast," the Inspector added. "That was a bit of luck."

The elderly doctor was there too.

"I had no idea when I admitted this patient that she was not your wife. Yesterday, my suspicions were aroused that some fraud was being perpetuated. I went to the police station this morning. It so happened that the police had had a message from Inspector Terry who had also received an enquiry about you. He came to Wimbledon immediately. Was the so-called clergyman a part of your gang? Was he here to establish if her memory had returned?"

"Oh no," Phoebe piped up suddenly. "He's a real clergyman, and a very dear friend of mine. In fact, we had an escape all arranged for tonight. Oh, this is going to be complicated now. I had everything planned! I was so looking forward to jumping from balcony to balcony, and he will be waiting for me at eleven outside the gate!"

The police were able to find Rev. Epworth at home in nearby Bromley, with Mr. Lionel Marshall, intending to catch the last train for Wimbledon. The two set out immediately to receive Phoebe into their care, and since it was still early, Lionel and Phoebe set out immediately for Blackbell Green. It was ten o'clock when they knocked on the door, and it was opened by Mr. Marshall, whose happiness knew no bounds.

Clara and her mother were utterly joyful to see Phoebe. Clara made a big pot of tea, and they sat around the table, drinking it and eating ginger biscuits, talking non-stop.

CHAPTER SIXTY-EIGHT

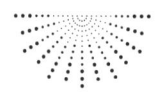

Lionel and Alice were wed in September and welcomed baby Richard the following July. Clara completed her nurse's training the following year, while Phoebe lived with their mother and father. Lewis called very often.

On a snowy day in January 1890, Clara and Thomas pledged themselves to each other forever, and Phoebe and Lewis did the same.

Aleksander brought his son over for a holiday the summer after that, and they stayed in the rectory in Bromley. Dora's grave was covered in flowers the entire summer. Clara added a bouquet too. No matter what she'd done, she did not deserve her early death and to miss her happy-ever-after with Aleksander.

THANK YOU FOR CHOOSING A PUREREAD BOOK!

We hope you enjoyed the story, and as a way to thank you for choosing PureRead we'd like to send you this free book, and other fun reader rewards…

Click here for your free copy of Whitechapel Waif
PureRead.com/victorian

Thanks again for reading.
See you soon!

LOVE VICTORIAN ROMANCE?

If you enjoyed this story why not continue straight away with other books in our PureRead Victorian Romance library?

Read them all...

Victorian Slum Girl's Dream

Poor Girl's Hope

The Lost Orphan of Cheapside

Born a Workhouse Baby

The Lowly Maid's Triumph

Poor Girl's Hope

The Victorian Millhouse Sisters

Dora's Workhouse Child

Saltwick River Orphan

Workhouse Girl and The Veiled Lady

OUR GIFT TO YOU

AS A WAY TO SAY THANK YOU WE WOULD LOVE TO SEND YOU THIS BEAUTIFUL STORY FREE OF CHARGE.

Click here for your free copy of Whitechapel Waif

PureRead.com/victorian

At PureRead we publish books you can trust. Great tales without smut or swearing, but with all of the mystery and romance you expect from a great story.

Be the first to know when we release new books, take part in our fun competitions, and get surprise free books in your inbox by signing up to our free VIP Reader list.

As a thank you you'll receive a copy of Whitechapel Waif straight away in you inbox.

Click here for your free copy of Whitechapel Waif

PureRead.com/victorian

Printed in Great Britain
by Amazon